THE BOYS OF SHILOH

JUNE HALL MCCASH

ISBN-13: 978-1-937937-14-0

First Edition

Printed in The United States of America

Twin Oaks Press
twinoakspress@gmail.com
www.twinoakspress.com

Design
Art Growden

To Luke and Ethan

*May this book be as close as
you ever come to war.*

THE SLEEPER IN THE VALLEY

There is a green hollow where a stream gurgles by,
wildly clutching at the grasses with its shreds
of silver, where the sun from the proud mountain
shines. It is a little valley bubbling with light.

A young soldier, open-mouthed, bareheaded,
the nape of his neck bathed in the cool, blue watercress,
sleeps. He is stretched out on the grass under the sky,
pale on his green bed where the light pours down.

His feet in the yellow gladioli, he sleeps. Smiling
as a sick child might smile; he is taking a nap.
Nature, cradle him warmly, for he is cold.

His nostrils do not quiver at the fragrance.
He sleeps in the sun, his hand on his chest,
peaceful. He has two red holes in his right side.

Arthur Rimbaud

*Arthur Rimbaud was a boy of sixteen, not much older than the boys in
the story you are about to read, when he wrote this sonnet. He too had
experienced the effects of war. The poem above is an English translation by
the author of this book. The original French version appears on the following
page. Poetry loses much of its music in translation. If you can find someone
to read it to you in French, you can listen to its original rhythms.*

Le Dormeur du Val

C'est un trou de verdure où chante une rivière,
Accrochant follement aux herbes des haillons
D'argent ; où le soleil, de la montagne fière,
Luit : c'est un petit val qui mousse de rayons.

Un soldat jeune, bouche ouverte, tête nue,
Et la nuque baignant dans le frais cresson bleu,
Dort ; il est étendu dans l'herbe, sous la nue,
Pâle dans son lit vert où la lumière pleut.

Les pieds dans les glaïeuls, il dort. Souriant comme
Sourirait un enfant malade, il fait un somme :
Nature, berce-le chaudement : il a froid.

Les parfums ne font pas frissonner sa narine ;
Il dort dans le soleil, la main sur sa poitrine,
Tranquille. Il a deux trous rouges au côté droit.

Arthur Rimbaud

TABLE OF CONTENTS

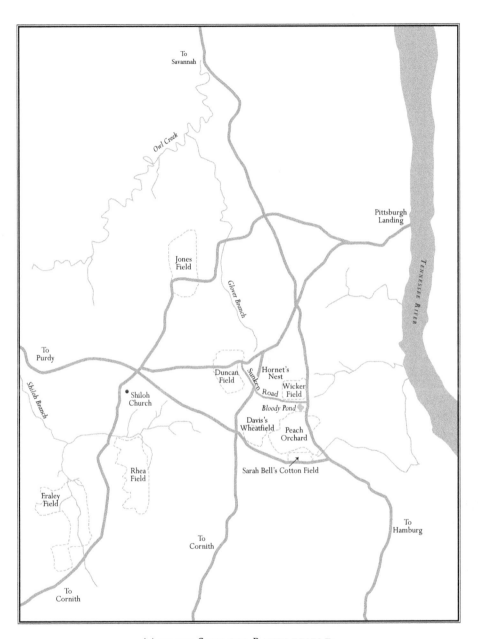

MAP OF SHILOH BATTLEFIELD

CHAPTER ONE

Luke

April 5, 1862, Shiloh, Tennessee

The boy rubbed a smooth stone with nervous fingers before he tossed it flat side downward toward the creek. He was trying to make it skip across the surface of the water like he used to do in the quiet pond of his daddy's pasture. A mockingbird sang from a nearby silver maple tree. It was the same call that trilled every morning in their peach orchard back home. He closed his eyes for a moment, listening, trying to make himself believe he was back there. But this was not home. And the creek was no still pond. The waters of Owl Creek tumbled restlessly over rocks and branches blocking its way. The boy felt as restless as the water, and tension seemed to hang in the air.

The narrow creek gurgled by. The boy watched it flow for a moment before he threw another stone. He knew there was no good way to skip stones in moving water, but he didn't much care. It was not the skipping, but the throwing of the stones, so hard and firm in his hand, that mattered. It was his way of trying to calm himself with something familiar and not be scared, to let himself pretend for a while that he was still on his family's South Georgia farm in the spring pasture, where the four milk cows would gather around the little pond to drink or lie in the shade of the live oak tree. Maybe he could even forget for a little while where he was now and what he had to do tomorrow.

The April air was warm and still, broken only by the nearby splashes of rocks hitting the water and the intermittent call of the mockingbird. In the distance he could hear an occasional echo of laughter from the camp to the east and a harmonica softly playing "Aura Lee." His mama liked that song and sometimes sang it as she scrubbed shirts and socks over the wash pot in the back yard. He could hear her voice in his mind:

> As the blackbird in the spring
> 'neath the willow tree
> sat and piped I heard him sing,
> praising Aura Lee.

Maybe, like the person in the lyrics, he was letting his imagination turn birdsong into a voice, his mother's voice, singing, a soothing, normal sound that drew his mind back to tranquil scenes of the pasture on his daddy's farm. Today, this peaceful place called Shiloh made him think of home.

Tomorrow, he knew, it would not be like this. But he planned to be brave and not fear the sound of drums and guns and the yells that would come from the throats of the men at his side. His captain had warned him what to expect. It would be his first battle, and he wanted to make his daddy proud. He wanted to run toward the enemy, whooping what the older soldiers called the Rebel yell. They'd heard that term from the Yankees and kind of liked it. They were proud that it scared the daylights out of Yankee soldiers, and they'd taught it to him back in Corinth, Mississippi, before the march to Tennessee, in case he ever got to fight. It wasn't hard to learn. It was just yelling like a wild animal.

Luke had turned thirteen just two days earlier. He knew he wasn't officially part of the army, but tomorrow they would need all the soldiers they could find to surprise and scare the Yankees. When he'd asked, even pleaded, to march with his older cousin Jimmy, who was a real soldier, the captain had hesitated only a moment before he'd agreed. Even so, he'd refused to put Luke's name on the roster. He told Jimmy to "keep an eye on the kid." Luke didn't like to hear himself called a kid. He thought at thirteen he was almost a man.

When he'd asked if he could get a uniform, the captain laughed and said he'd try to find him a cap at least, maybe even a jacket. But he pointed out that many of the soldiers didn't have proper uniforms, so Luke wouldn't look any different from a lot of them.

Today he might still be just a boy in a torn gray shirt and rough trousers, faded to a nondescript color and fastened at the waist with a worn, hand-me-down belt that once belonged to his cousin Jimmy. But tomorrow Luke too would be a soldier.

Jimmy was five years older than Luke. At eighteen, he had enlisted in the regiment only a short time before. He even had his own musket, brought all the way from Waycross, Georgia. That's where both Luke and Jimmy came from and where their families lived. When Jimmy had told Luke that he was leaving Waycross to find General Johnston's army in Mississippi and join up with the Confederates, Luke had begged to come along. Jimmy had finally agreed, but convincing Luke's parents had been a lot harder.

Luke's daddy said that he was too young to fight and that the army probably wouldn't let him carry a gun, despite the fact that he was a good shot and went hunting every fall with his uncles and cousins. He couldn't play a drum or anything like that, but after he'd begged a while longer, his daddy had finally said maybe he could help out around the camp or serve as messenger. He said he didn't want his boy fighting just to take his daddy's place.

His daddy wanted to join the army himself, but he couldn't fight because he had injured his leg four years earlier when his horse had stumbled and fallen on him. Now he walked with a stick. But Luke felt that his daddy, despite his objections, in his heart was right proud that his son would want to go and do his part. Neither his mama nor his daddy was happy about Jimmy and Luke going all the way to Mississippi to join up. They thought Jimmy could surely have enlisted in a unit in Georgia. But he seemed determined to join the troops under the command of General Albert Sidney Johnston, who, he'd heard from a passing stranger, was now massing troops at Corinth, Mississippi, for a major attack on the Yankees. With him was General Beauregard who had whipped the Yankees so gloriously at Manassas the year before. Jimmy was determined to sign up with them.

Luke remembered how his mother was crying when he left the farm. He'd felt bad about making her cry. She'd clutched him round the neck to hold him back, making his sandy hair fall into his eyes. His mama's words echoed in his head, as he and Jimmy were heading out, "Now, son, you be careful. I don't want you out there gettin' shot at." She hadn't wanted him to go at all, and she'd cried and cried, wiping her eyes with her apron. But he was pretty sure his daddy understood.

"You're too young to go to war, Luke," she said over and over. "Let Jimmy go. He's old enough, I reckon, but you stay here. We need you to tend the crops and look after the cows."

But Luke knew that his daddy, in spite of his bad leg, still took care of those things. Besides, his little brother Billy was nine now, old enough to help more than he already did. And they had the colored man everyone in the family called "Uncle John" to help out, though he was old now and spent most of his days sitting in front of his cabin, whittling whistles out of reeds for children who lived in cabins like his on other nearby farms. But he could still milk a cow and feed chickens and do light work around the house. They would get along just fine. Luke felt like it was his duty to go, since his daddy couldn't.

When they'd finally said all their goodbyes, Jimmy and Luke had set out on their long voyage to Corinth, the longest of Luke's life. He wasn't used to sleeping in barns or open fields as they had to do during their voyage. They'd packed as much food as they could carry, but when that ran out, they had to depend on whatever they could forage in the fields or whatever a kind farmer's wife was willing to share with them. He remembered one really special Sunday when a sweet-faced lady gave them fried chicken legs and two boiled eggs. Once they'd eaten and set out again, one of her boys came running after them to deliver two large slices of jam cake. "Mama said to tell you she forgot dessert." That was the best meal they had during the whole trip.

They'd walked all the way to Macon, except when they could hitch a ride on the back of some farmer's wagon. There they'd come across a railroad line that seemed to be going in the right direction and followed the tracks a few miles until they were able to hop on a passing train. But the line did not go all the way. They made it on the train only as far as Montgomery, Alabama. From there they walked, hitched rides, and took ferries to Meridian, Mississippi. From Meridian, they were able to ride a flatcar on the Mobile and Ohio Railroad all the rest of the way. The trip took twelve days in all, but when they finally reached the railroad junction at Corinth, they found a camp full of impatient soldiers chomping at the bit to fight the Yankees.

General Johnston was there, just like they'd heard, making plans with General Beauregard and the other officers. By the time Luke and Jimmy got to Corinth, everything was almost ready. The generals had rolled up their maps and were preparing to get their troops on the road. The soldiers, who weren't supposed to know the plans, told Jimmy that they'd heard they were going north to Tennessee, where Yankee soldiers were supposed to be camped along the Tennessee River.

As soon as they'd reached Corinth, Jimmy had enlisted and signed the rosters, but the sergeant-in-charge wouldn't sign Luke up. He said he was too young. Luke tried to tell him he'd be thirteen in just a few days. The sergeant didn't seem interested, but when Jimmy explained how far they'd come and how far it was back to the boy's home, the sergeant said, "Well, I reckon he can tag along and do odd jobs around the camp or maybe help the cooks or something. But I can't put him on the roster, and we ain't gonna pay him."

Luke was really glad they hadn't turned him away.

He and Jimmy had arrived in Corinth just in time before the army began its march toward Tennessee. They had only half a day of rest before they had to begin another long trek. But this was what they had come for.

Slogging for days through the early spring rain and mud, they had followed what seemed at times to be only a cow path, but which the captain called Ridge Road. Blue and white wildflowers bloomed alongside the ruts of the roadway, and every now and again, they passed a pretty girl or two standing behind a fence, waving handkerchiefs and smiling at the passing troops. Jimmy always waved and smiled back, but Luke just felt his face turn red, and he fixed his eyes on the road.

After two more days of marching in April downpours and along muddy roads, the weary soldiers finally reached their destination and set up camp. Rumors passed among the troops that tomorrow morning they were going to make a surprise attack on the Yankees camped along the river and out of sight on the other side of a ridge, near a little building called Shiloh Church and Purdy Road.

So far, in his few days with the army, Luke had mostly done errands, hauling water buckets, feeding horses, helping the cook serve up meals, and carrying notes to officers from one side of the camp to another. But tomorrow would be different. Now that he was really thirteen, the captain had overruled the sergeant and given him permission to march alongside Jimmy, who'd already been named corporal and was assigned to accompany the man carrying the battle flag for their battalion in the attack tomorrow. If the flagbearer fell, Jimmy was to take up the flag. And if Jimmy fell, Luke was to find someone to hoist it once again. Jimmy might even let Luke carry his rifle and his ammunition.

The boy felt really proud and important. Like the others, he would go into battle with the advance forces. He would let out that war whoop to scare the enemy, that Confederate yell he'd learned. And he would be a man and make his daddy proud. He felt it in his heart. He was trying really hard not to be scared.

As he bent down to pick up another stone, he caught sight of a shadow moving in the late afternoon sun on the other side of the creek.

CHAPTER TWO

Luke / Ethan

As Luke stood up, he saw the shadow move again. His heart was beating fast, but he set his jaw, determined not to show fear.

"I see you," he called out in the bravest voice he could muster. "You might as well come out in the open." He could see something or someone crouching behind a persimmon bush, and then a flash of blue ducked into the pine thicket.

"What's the matter? You scared or somethin'?" Luke taunted him again.

A dark-haired boy not much taller than himself, but thin and lanky, stepped out from behind a tree and ran his fingers through his dark hair. "I ain't scared of nothing," he shouted back. "Certainly not you, Reb."

Luke was on the alert now. He knew that the boy on the other side of the creek must be from the Yankee camp. There weren't any other troops, as far as he knew, in this part of Tennessee. The boy didn't look mean and devilish, like he'd heard the Yankees were.

"What's your name?" Luke called out.

"Ethan," said the boy from across the creek. "What's yours?"

"Luke," he called back. "Where you from?"

"None of your business."

"Well, okay then. Who cares anyway?" Luke tossed a jagged stone into the creek.

"Bet I can throw farther than you!" Ethan challenged.

"Bet you can't!" Luke picked up another rock and threw it as hard as he could. It landed on the other side of the creek several yards beyond the boy in blue.

"Why don't you come on over here and let's see," the boy hollered.

Luke was immediately apprehensive. But the boy on the other side of the creek seemed to think he was just a Tennessee farm kid, not a soldier as he would be tomorrow. He could tell from his voice that the boy over there was a Yankee. Still, his honor was challenged, and he couldn't pass up a good contest.

He took off his brogans and socks, left them on the bank, and set out to cross the creek stepping from stone to stone. Halfway, his foot slipped on a mossy rock, and he found himself sitting upright in the cold water. The boy in blue started to laugh.

"Clumsy!" he called. But the day was warm and the water looked good. He sat down and took off his shoes, rolled up his pants leg, and waded out into the middle of the little creek. Luke splashed water toward the Yankee boy, who splashed back. Both boys were laughing now.

"Hey, look! There's a fish! Bet I can catch it with my bare hands," said Ethan.

"Bet you can't!" Luke answered. And suddenly both boys were squatting in the water lunging for the small, silvery fish swimming in the eddy.

When they were both tired and soaking wet, the fish having eluded their clutches, they scrambled up onto Ethan's side of the creek bank, and stretched out in the last warm rays of the sun to dry.

"I bet you're with those Yankee soldiers camped over the ridge there," Luke said.

"Am not. I'm here to visit my grandmother," Ethan lied. "Ain't no Yankee soldiers over there anyway."

"Is your grandma a Yankee?"

"What makes you think I'm a Yankee?"

Luke burst out laughing. "Lordamercy. The way you talk. Don't nobody down here talk like that."

"You won't tell anybody, will you? I'm not supposed to leave the camp."

"Heck no! Who would I tell anyway?" He gestured toward the empty fields.

"You got any brothers or sisters?" Ethan asked.

"One brother, younger 'n me. What about you?"

"Two older sisters. Real pests. Be glad you have a brother."

"Yeah, I guess. But he's only nine and not much good for nothin'."

"At least he's a boy."

"Yeah." Luke loved the feel of the sun on his face. He thought about Billy and all the times he had been in the way. But now he'd give just about anything to see him again. Billy wasn't such a bad kid, but the way he imitated everything Luke did just about drove him crazy. Every time he complained about it, his mama said imitation was the sincerest form of flattery, whatever that meant. He'd puzzled over it a while before he asked her. She said it meant that Billy wanted to be like him. Secretly he kind of liked it now that he thought about it a little bit.

"Where you from up North?" Luke asked, putting a blade of grass between his teeth and biting down to taste the green spring juice.

"Illinois—near Springfield. Ever been up there?"

"Naw, my folks don't travel much. Been to Atlanta though. And Mississippi," he added, glancing over at Ethan to see if he was beginning to figure things out, but he was staring up at the sky, trying to see shapes in the clouds.

"You ever been South before?" Luke asked.

"Nope, first time. But it's right pretty here."

"Well, it's best in the spring, but it gets mighty hot in the summer."

"I just might come back some time and see for myself."

"You do that, but just remember, I told you so. Yankee boy like

13

you'd just melt away in the summer sun."

"And you'd never survive our snow, I bet," Ethan hesitated. "You ever been sledding?"

Luke laughed. Sledding in South Georgia was a funny thought. He'd read about stuff like that at school, but it hardly ever snowed where he lived, and when it did it hardly ever stuck. "Don't reckon so. What's it like?"

"Like flying. You come down those icy hills just flying. Nothing like it. Come on up to Illinois next winter, and I'll show you."

"'At's a great idea!" said Luke enthusiastically. Then he thought about it for a minute. "But what about this war?"

"Aw, it'll be over by then. We're going to whip you Rebs up one side and down the other," said Ethan.

"I don't reckon you will," Luke answered with quiet determination.

"Well ... maybe not." Ethan deflected any annoyance he had caused in Luke with laughter. "You Rebs do fight pretty good."

"You ever been in a battle?" Luke asked.

"A couple of times." Ethan's voice was almost a whisper.

"Were you scared?"

"I ... Not exactly," said Ethan, looking intently at the sky, searching the clouds.

"Well, I wouldn't be scared," Luke boasted.

"Are you sure?" Ethan looked at him now. "Real sure?"

"Naw, not me. I've faced some pretty tough bullies in my day.

One in the school yard and once out behind the church. Gave that one a bloody nose. I ain't scared of nobody."

"Let's see how tough you are." Ethan rolled over on his stomach, leaned on his elbows, and stretched out one hand to Luke. "Want to arm wrestle?"

"Sure, why not?" Luke maneuvered himself into position and took Ethan's hand in his. The two boys tugged and grunted.

Finally, Luke said, "Look out. They's a wasp in your hair!"

Ethan let go and swatted at his head.

"I win!" Luke announced triumphantly.

"Hey, no fair. There wasn't no wasp."

"I win anyway. Anyone dumb enough to fall for that ol' trick deserves to lose."

Ethan shoved Luke's shoulder, and suddenly the two boys were tussling energetically in the grass, but it was only a half-hearted skirmish. Ethan wasn't really mad, just annoyed with himself for biting at Luke's bait.

"You wrestle pretty good—for a Yank," Luke admitted when they were both tired of the game and lay back on the grass again.

"You too," Ethan said. "For a Reb, I mean."

The two boys stared up at the sky in silence for a while. Luke thought he saw an elephant in the scudding clouds and tried to point it out to Ethan, who didn't see it at all. "Looks like a cow to me."

"You ever see a cow with a trunk like 'at?"

15

"I don't see a trunk." Luke tried his best to point it out, but Ethan couldn't seem to see anything but a cow. Both boys stared at the sky a while longer, searching for images.

Finally, Luke sat up and hugged his knees. "What you think this war is all about anyhow?"

"My pa said it was 'cause you Rebs won't free your slaves."

"Free 'em from what?" Luke asked.

"You know. Bondage. Captivity. Like Moses's people."

"Oh."

"You got any slaves?" Ethan asked.

"I don't think so …, 'cept, I guess, maybe Uncle John," Luke replied, after thinking about it for a while. "I reckon he's a slave."

"You have an uncle who's a slave?"

"Well, he's not really my uncle."

"Why do you call him uncle?"

"We just do. Everybody does that where I come from. If a colored man gets real old and he's been with your fam'ly a long time, we call 'im uncle."

"Why?"

"Just to make 'im feel like part of the fam'ly, I guess."

"That's dumb."

"Well, that's what we do anyhow. He's been on the farm ever since I was born. Him and Aunt Mattie. That was his wife. She died two summers ago, and Uncle John's been real sad ever since."

"Don't they have any children?"

"I heard 'im talk about a son once, but he was gone 'fore I was born."

"'Spect he got sold off."

"I dunno. I ain't never seen 'im."

"That'd be awful, getting sold off from your pa and ma."

"Yeah, it would," agreed Luke, remembering his own parents, the familiar, savory smells from his mother's kitchen, and the warmth of the wood fire his daddy built in the stove every winter morning before he got dressed. He couldn't imagine life without them.

"What kind of work does he do?" asked Ethan.

"Who?"

"Uncle John."

"Not much of nothin' anymore. He used to help daddy on the farm. 'Bout all he does now is feed the chickens and milk the cows. Sometimes he helps Mama shuck the corn or bring in a little firewood. Mostly just whittles."

"Whittles?"

"Yeah, you know, makes them little whistles out of reeds for the colored children down the road."

"Oh," said Ethan. He thought for a minute, then, leaning on one elbow and looking intently at Luke. "Does your pa beat him?"

"Beat him? Why would he do that?"

"My pa showed me pictures one time of a slave that'd been whipped real bad. Said that's why we're fighting this war, so everybody can be free and people can't do that any more."

"Why would anyone want to beat somebody who helped 'em out around the place?"

"I don't know, but they do."

"Well, I guess I've heard about it too." He hesitated. "Fact is, I saw a man whipped once," Luke admitted.

"What had he done?"

"Stole a ham from the smokehouse up at the Potter place."

"What was it like?"

"Man, it was bad. He cried and begged and whimpered, but ol' man Potter jest whipped 'im harder. He got cut up pretty bad. But he shouldn't've stole. The Bible says 'Thou shalt not steal.'"

"Maybe he was hungry."

"Maybe. I couldn't say. Mr. Potter was mighty mad though. Still, I reckon he oughtn't to have whipped 'im like 'at." The boys sat silent for a spell.

"Your Uncle John, does he eat with you folks?"

Luke laughed. "Heck no. He wouldn't do that .... Mama takes him his supper down to the cabin sometimes if we have leftovers, or else he fries up a little bacon and mush, sometimes eggs and stuff from the garden for his other meals. Sometimes I go down to the cabin and eat with him. But Mama and Daddy wouldn't do that."

"They don't mind if you do?"

"Naw. Me and Billy, we been goin' down there since we was little kids, so Uncle John can tell us stories. He knows a lot of good stories, and he tells 'em real funny."

"What kind of stories?" Ethan asked.

"Oh, you know, stories about Brer Rabbit outfoxin' folks, like when he pretends to be scared of the briar patch. Or when he ties Brer Tiger to a tree so he won't blow away. Ever'body knows those stories 'round here."

"Never heard them myself."

"Well, you just come on down here, and we'll let you get an education," Luke said, laughing. "Cain't nobody tell 'em like Uncle John," he mused. "I sure do miss 'im."

"Doesn't he live around here?"

Luke realized that he had just slipped up and nearly given away the fact that Tennessee was not his home. He thought furiously. "Well … right now he's sick, and Mama don't like me to go down there 'cause she's a-feared we might ketch it."

"What's he got?"

"You sure do ask a lot of questions. … I think I better get goin'. It's gittin' late, and supper'll be ready soon."

"Where's your farm?"

"Over yonder a ways," Luke gestured noncommittally toward the direction from which he had come. He felt bad lying to Ethan, but he knew he couldn't give away the fact that he was with a Confederate battalion beyond the wooded hill to the south. A lot was at risk—that he understood. But he felt right bad anyway. He'd been taught not to tell lies. "Well, I gotta go."

"Aw, do you have to?"

"Well, I gotta clean my rifle," Luke said boastfully. "I'm going huntin' tomorrow with my cousin Jimmy." He was playing with Ethan now and feeling almost guilty about it.

"You got a rifle?"

"Well, a musket. It's really my cousin Jimmy's, but he lets me use it sometimes. You ain't got a rifle? What do you do in that Yankee army anyway?"

"I'm a drummer boy."

"Where'd you learn to play a drum?"

"My pa taught me. He used to play with a marching band up in Springfield."

"Must be fun bein' a drummer," said Luke, with a pause. Then he asked, "Where's your pa now?"

Ethan didn't say anything for a few seconds, and Luke could see him blinking back tears.

"He got killed in Missouri last November, at a place called Belmont, not far from Cairo." Ethan paused for a moment and swallowed hard, then added, "Mama wanted me to come home and stay after that, but I just couldn't. I thought I needed to be with the army for Pa's sake."

"I'm real sorry," said Luke, not knowing what else to say.

Both boys were silent for a long while, thinking their own thoughts and feeling rather awkward with each other, but feeling right close too. Luke thought it must be just awful to lose one's daddy like that. And he knew that some Confederate soldier had probably shot him. But he didn't know what to say to Ethan. Finally he broke the quiet. "Well, I reckon I better get goin'."

"Yeah. I wish ya didn't have to. You think we could get together tomorrow?"

"Sure, why not? As my daddy always says, 'God willin' and the creek don't rise.'" That meant that his intentions were good. But Luke knew better than Ethan that God might not be willing. It all depended on the battle, which he knew about but Ethan didn't. The Yankees had no idea they were about to be attacked. Luke felt kind of bad about it, considering Ethan's pa and all.

"Well, I guess I'll see you then. Okay?"

"Okay, I hope so." And he did hope so. Luke rose, rolled up his still damp pants legs, and waded carefully back across the creek, not wanting to risk slipping on the mossy stones again.

"It was good to meet ya," Ethan yelled after Luke had put on his socks and brogans and waved good-bye.

"You too. Real good."

Luke trudged back up the low hill on his side of the creek and turned once more at the crest to wave at Ethan, but the boy was gone. He had slipped back into the woods to join his unit, which Luke knew from soldiers' prattle was camped somewhere near the Tennessee River not far from a place called Pittsburgh Landing. Luke stood there, looking out over the meadow, the creek, and the pine thicket beyond, wondering about the boy he had just met. He seemed real nice. He reminded Luke of Noah Willingham, one of the boys who had been in his class back when he was in school. He'd always liked Noah. He was a friend you could trust.

All of a sudden, Luke felt a wave of homesickness sweep over him, and for some reason he didn't want the afternoon to end. It felt like the end of some special part of his life, the significance of which he couldn't quite unravel.

The sun was getting lower on the horizon now, and he knew he'd better get back to camp before Jimmy got worried about him. Tomorrow was his first battle, he thought, and he was going to march beside the flag bearer and maybe even carry Jimmy's gun and ammunition. Today he was just a boy, but tomorrow he would be a soldier who would do his best and make his daddy proud.

CHAPTER THREE

Ethan

As he walked carefully through the cotton field, where leafy plants in neat rows were just peeking green above the earth, Ethan thought about the farm boy he had just met. *Luke.* He liked the name. It would be kind of fun to come back to Tennessee and visit sometime. Sometime when there was no war. He figured that if he came in the summer, even if it was really hot, they could find a swimming hole somewhere or a fishing pole. He remembered how he and Luke had lunged, trying to catch the silvery fish in the creek he had just left. The fish were small, but there were probably bigger ones in there. Even better, they could take their poles to the nearby Tennessee River. It would be fun to go fishing again. He hadn't been fishing since the war started. Not since his pa died. He wondered if he would ever get a chance to go again.

He hurried back across the greening, well-tended fields until he reached the road that led toward Pittsburgh Landing and his unit's campsite. He wanted to make sure he got back to camp in time for supper and before anyone missed him. Nobody would come looking for him, he expected, unless one of the other drummer boys wanted to play cards or something. But they wouldn't be surprised if he wasn't in his tent. All the boys wandered around the camp when drills were over for the afternoon. They ran errands for the officers or just did what everyone else was doing, crouching around the campfire with the other soldiers, talking, telling stories, or listening to the harmonica players pass the time with their tunes.

The troops drilled mostly in the mornings, but by late afternoon they usually sat around with their sleeves rolled up, shirts unbuttoned at the neck, just waiting—waiting, Ethan supposed, for General Buell's troops to arrive from Nashville and join in some rumored march against the Rebs. Ethan wasn't sure what the destination was to be, but he had been catching snatches of conversation among the officers who talked about a massed march somewhere. And he'd heard all sorts of rumors from the troops around the camp. They were all eager for another victory.

When the war first started a year ago, the federal troops were surprised by the ferocity and determination with which the Confederate forces fought. The Union had suffered an especially humiliating defeat at the Battle of Manassas the year before, and for a time, it had demoralized the northern troops. But with Grant now in command, a string of Union victories since the beginning of the year, especially the Battles of Fort Henry and Fort Donelson in February, and then the fall of Nashville, had given them heart again. Now they wanted another win. They all thought that with a major victory, maybe they could bring this war to a quick end. Ethan hoped they were right.

He stopped from time to time to gaze back at the sunset, reflected so vividly in the wispy clouds. The world looked orderly, with the fields all plowed in even rows and cherry and peach orchards, which seemed almost white earlier in the day, now glowing vivid pink with blossoms that mirrored the colors of the afternoon. Everything was so peaceful and beautiful that he wanted this day to linger on.

By the time he got back to his unit's campsite, the sun had almost completely sunk below the horizon. The troops were already lined up to fill their tin plates with what the men liked to called "grub." He hurried back to his tent to get his own plate and fork.

"Where you been, boy?" the fat cook asked, as he dished up Ethan's unidentifiable meat and overcooked potatoes. "All you drummer boys are usually first in line."

"Oh, been around, here and there," Ethan answered with a shrug. He didn't want to tell anyone he had sneaked out of camp just to get away for a while. The cook said nothing, just nodded and turned away to dish up the meal for the next soldier in line.

Unlike a lot of boys, Ethan always liked to spend time alone. It was not unusual for him to find a quiet spot somewhere under a tree by himself or in a sunny patch of purple and yellow flowers the soldiers called Johnny Jump-ups, where he could forget the war for a few minutes and simply watch the birds and squirrels playing around the edges of the woods. Ever since his pa's death, those quiet moments when he could be by himself seemed to be more necessary. He didn't want to show the extent of his sadness in front of the other soldiers. But sometimes it overwhelmed him, and he just needed to get away.

He missed his whole family being together. He knew they would never all be together again, not like before, now that his father was gone. But he would like to see his mother again, and he was determined he would put up with her hugs without his usual protests. He would probably hug her back. He had to admit that he even looked forward to seeing his sisters again. *They aren't nearly as pesky as I make out,* he thought to himself, though he would never have admitted it to Luke.

Ethan would be glad when this war was over. Everybody seemed certain that it wouldn't last too many more months. In the beginning, the Union troops, who had not expected the Rebs to have such courage and fighting skills, had learned to be better prepared and to train harder.

Now that the tide had turned a bit, General Grant, whom Ethan thought of as the leader of the northern army and whose headquarters were in a fancy house across the river at a place called Savannah, seemed certain that the Union would soon prevail. And General Sherman, who was encamped up near a log building they called Shiloh Church, agreed. At least that's what they told the troops, who wanted more than anything to believe them.

General Wallace, who had recently been promoted and now headed up Ethan's division, kept reassuring his men it would soon be over as well. At the outset of the war, soldiers enlisted for only three months. Everyone seemed to think it would be long enough to bring fighting to an end. But when the three months were up and the war continued on, the army had to recruit more men or reenlist the same ones over again. Now men were enlisting for three years, but nobody would mind going home early.

The generals, Ethan learned when he returned to camp, had all spent the afternoon at the campsite of General Sherman. Ethan figured they were planning what he'd come to think of as "the Big March."

General Wallace rode in on his horse about suppertime, not long after Ethan's return, and informed his troops that everything was quiet. He said he'd found General Sherman "in fine spirits" and eager for the arrival of Buell's troops. Though he didn't say it out loud, Ethan finished the thought in his own mind with "and planning the Big March against the Confederates." He wondered when and where it would take place.

When he finished his supper, Ethan sat around the campfire with the other men for a while, listening to soldiers play their harmonicas, while others sang the popular songs of the day. Some of the ones the men seemed to like best were "John Brown's Body" and the newer song with the same tune, "The Battle Hymn of the Republic." They were easy to play and easy to sing, and they seemed to stir up the men with the righteousness of their cause. Others sat in their tents, lanterns lit, playing cards or writing letters until the stars came out and the moon rose over the horizon and shone through the feathery clouds that drifted by.

As the evening grew darker, the songs got sadder, and some of the soldiers grew misty-eyed. Ethan usually drifted away when the sad songs began. He could hear the men's voices echoing the choruses through the night, as he walked away from the firelight toward his tent. The voices were fewer now, for not everyone knew the lyrics to some of the newer songs, but they learned to join in the chorus:

> *Brave boys are they!*
> *Gone at their country's call;*
> *And yet, and yet we cannot forget*
> *That many brave boys must fall.*

Ethan crept into his tent, leaving the flap open. He liked to lie in the darkness, gazing out at the blinking stars and letting the voices of the soldiers lull him to sleep with their melodies. If tears sometimes came to his eyes before he fell asleep, he could blink them away or let them roll down his cheeks. No one else would ever know.

CHAPTER FOUR

Luke

April 6, 1862, Confederate Camp

It was Sunday morning. The sun, barely peeking over the horizon, shone red through the trees like a distant fire. Luke woke with a start at the sound of a single voice and peered out of his tent. One of the soldiers, a preacher in civilian life, he supposed, was holding up a Bible and praying aloud, though not as loud as some of the revival preachers Luke had heard back in Waycross.

"Lord, give us the courage to do what we've come here to do. Keep us safe if it be your will. And Lord, protect our loved ones at home," he intoned. A man from Alabama, Luke guessed from his accent.

Some of the soldiers hovered around him with their heads bowed. Several knelt on one knee, using their muskets or rifles to steady them. Some of them said, "Amen." Others were paying no mind, but slurped on the bitter coffee the cook had tried to brew by pouring cold water over ground-up chicory. From the looks of the soldiers' faces, Luke thought, it must not be too good. Some of the men were chewing on hardtack and dried salted beef from their haversacks. The officers wouldn't let them light cookfires, which might attract the attention of the enemy who, rumor had it, were camped about two miles away with their backs to the river. The soldiers held their weapons in their hands or had propped them against nearby trees. Some had their bayonets already fixed. The men looked nervous. Their jaws were set and their eyes narrowed. They knew what lay ahead.

Luke laced up his brogans and scrambled to his feet. His heart lurched as he too remembered what the day held—his first battle. He looked about for his cousin Jimmy, whose bedding lay rolled up beside his own. Jimmy stood among the huddle of praying men, his eyes closed as the preacher asked God for victory in the battle to come.

Luke scurried into a grove of trees to relieve himself. By the time he got back the praying was done, and the white-faced men were stamping nervously about or squatting under trees holding their guns and waiting for orders.

"'Bout time you woke up, buddy," Jimmy said to Luke with a smile as the boy emerged from the woods, buttoning his fly. "Here,

eat some of this Johnny cake. It's kinda stale but better 'n nothin'."
He held out a slice of the yellow cornmeal cake to Luke.

Luke took it and munched on it hungrily. He had some beef jerky
left in his haversack and chewed on that as well, washing it down
with water from his canteen.

Jimmy spoke quietly to his younger cousin, talking to him for
the first time like he was really grown up. "You remember the plan
we talked about. You'll be my gun bearer if I need one. We'll run
alongside the flag-bearer. If he's hit, I'll pick up the flag and give you
my gun to tote. Now hustle, boy, we don't wanna get left behind.
And you gotta keep up."

Luke nodded, already feeling the need to pee again.

"It's okay, Luke," Jimmy said, looking at his tense face. "You'll
be fine." He gave the boy an encouraging pat on the shoulder. "Your
daddy would be proud."

Luke grinned, but he didn't feel nearly as confident as he tried to
look. He reached into his pocket to make sure his lucky agate marble
was there. His grandfather had sent it to him from Germany, and he'd
won lots of games using it as his shooter. It always brought him luck.
Holding its smooth round surface with his fingers, he also said a little
silent prayer to God. He feared he might need them both today.

General Johnston galloped into their encampment on horseback
with several other officers who had spent much of the night fine-

tuning their strategy. The men lined up and stood at attention, waiting for his command. Sitting astride his bay stallion Fire Eater, who looked as proud as his rider, the middle-aged general was an awesome sight. As he reviewed the field of soldiers, all eyes were turned in his direction. He was a big man, over six feet, as best Luke could judge. He wore a handlebar moustache, and his dark hair grew down around his ears. He looked calm, but his eyes were fever bright as he faced the troops.

He sat tall in his saddle as he spoke, reiterating some of the things the captain had already said to them the night before, about fighting the invaders of our country and the need to protect their mothers and sisters from the Yankee horde and to march to a "decisive victory." Some of the men weren't so sure, as the dark night breeze had carried occasional sounds of Union soldiers near the river singing marching songs and cheering. They feared the Yankees might already know the Confederates were nearby and were preparing for an attack.

But the general looked confident and determined. To his words he added a new note of certainty to hearten his troops: "Tonight," he said, "we will water our horses in the Tennessee River."

The beefy-faced captain who commanded their unit hurried toward them. "It's time, men," he said. "Let's go. Line up, and let's march. Be quick and be quiet. We wanna catch those Yanks with their pants down. Now follow me."

The men formed a ragged line and started to march as noiselessly as possible through the woods, tangled with briars and low-growing vines. There was no drumbeat, no sound of a bugle, which Luke had expected. It was all quiet, at least as quiet as thousands of men could ever be as they stumbled through the thick underbrush.

Jimmy hurried alongside the flag-bearer, a stocky man in his late thirties who set his bearded chin with determination and strode as fast as he could through the trees. It was not easy with the flag held aloft, and he was already dipping it to avoid low-hanging branches. For more than a mile they marched wordlessly through woods and clearings until they reached a small ridge. In the valley below, Luke could see in the distance a little creek like the one where he'd met Ethan the day before. Through another copse of trees, he could make out occasional white dots that he thought must be tents. Finally, they were in sight of the enemy.

Once more General Johnston rode past his men, encouraging them and urging them to "fire low." Suddenly Luke heard the sound of gunfire, and at his captain's signal, everyone began to run forward.

"On the quickstep, men. When you can see 'em, let 'em hear you. And if it's dressed in blue, shoot it," the captain shouted.

Yells and shots came from up ahead. The battle had begun.

CHAPTER FIVE

Luke

As they started to run, Luke heard the men all around him yelling at the top of their lungs. They sounded like a bunch of banshees or a pack of wolves. He could see why it might scare the enemy. Luke began his run alongside Jimmy as they raced toward the Yankee camp. He could feel his heart thudding with excitement.

Union troops were scurrying about in confusion. As the Confederates stormed into their campground, they could see it littered with soapy shaving brushes, washbasins, and overturned coffee pots—signs of all the things the Yankees had been doing before the attack.

Blue-clad soldiers, some still in undershirts or unbuttoned jackets with their underwear showing beneath, snatched up their weapons and were beginning to fire at the running men. The flag-bearer suddenly dropped to his knees. A minié ball had pierced his belly. Jimmy grabbed the flag before it hit the ground. Without stopping he ran on through the Union camp. It was all Luke could do to keep up with him. He was carrying Jimmy's musket now, eager for an opportunity to stop and shoot.

The ground up ahead was already strewn with the bodies of men, some in blue, some in gray. The dead and wounded seemed to be everywhere. Blood was gushing from their arms or legs or streaming down their faces. Moans of the wounded were drowned out by the shrill sounds Luke heard coming from his own throat, in echo of the other men in his unit.

They made it to the other side of the camp, where Jimmy stopped and turned around to wave the flag at the Yankees. The men who had run all the way through the camp were now stopping to regroup in the safety of the woods on the other side, as the officers on horseback were shouting commands. Luke could feel his heart beating fast and his teeth chattering, while minié balls continued to hit the trees all around them.

Jimmy grinned at him. "We made it, buddy," he said to Luke.

Just then, a shot rang out, louder than the rest. Luke saw Jimmy's eyes roll back in his head. Blood spurted from his left temple.

"Jimmy, Jimmy!" he screamed, dropping to his knees beside his fallen cousin, whose legs still twitched on the ground. Soldiers kept running past Luke, blurs of gray as he knelt beside Jimmy's body and tried to breathe again. The moment seemed unreal, as though time had stopped. He stared at Jimmy's face. His eyes were still open in surprise.

"Get that flag off the ground, boy." A voice growled in his ear, and a rough hand punched at his shoulder. Luke turned to look up into the eyes of a grizzled man, his face lined with cracks and dirt. Luke reached out to pick up the flag lying beside his cousin. Tears were streaming down his face. He brushed his running nose with his sleeve and wiped away the tears with his fingers. The man spat on the ground, before taking a closer look at Luke.

"I'll take it, boy. I reckon you're too young to tote it," he said in a quieter voice, wresting the flag from Luke's hands. Carrying the battle flag was a dangerous assignment, for the bearer was always a target for Union fire.

Luke didn't resist, but watched the man raise the flag high and turn back in the direction of the enemy, yelling as he went. Still crouched beside Jimmy's body, he felt his face grow hot with shame that he hadn't caught the flag before it fell to the dirt as Jimmy had done. He'd failed in his duty as a soldier, and he bit his lip until he could taste blood at his own ineptness. He felt a sudden urge to kill the man who'd shot his cousin, whoever it was. He snatched up Jimmy's gun again and unhooked the cartridge box from his still body.

Luke ran toward the thick of the fighting and began to fire as often as he could reload. He couldn't tell through the hot tears that filled his eyes whether he was hitting anyone or not, but he fired at the running Yankees again and again and again until he had no more ammunition.

He found a gray-clad body lying face down beside a tree, bleeding from a gaping hole in the back. He eyed the man's cartridge box, but he hesitated for a moment. He didn't like touching the body, as though it might rise up and accuse him of stealing. His mother's voice rang in his ears, as clearly as if she were standing by his side, "Thou shalt not steal," but the man couldn't ever use it again, so Luke took what was left of the soldier's ammunition. Throughout the morning and into the afternoon he tried to keep up with the soldiers in the ranks, and, like everyone else, he shot at any blue figure he saw, barely taking time to aim, as long as his ammunition held out.

Throughout the afternoon the men rushed through the woods to get to the next open field where they would form a new line of attack. Except for the furious gunfire, it was a beautiful afternoon. Wildflowers of all kinds—violets, black-eyed Susans, and red cardinal flowers—dotted the woods and clearings. During the skirmishes, the sweet spring air had given way to the acrid smell of gunpowder. It was a familiar odor by now. During intermittent silences, Luke could hear an occasional bird chirp, though it was rare. Most of the birds had flown away.

By the position of the sun, Luke judged it to be after two o'clock.

He suddenly realized how tired and hungry he was. No Yankee soldiers were in sight, and the men around him seemed to be pausing for a brief rest, so he sat down under a tree and opened his haversack to rummage for any stale bread or dried beef it might yet contain.

He was chewing on the tough meat when a red-faced young soldier came half-trotting, half-stumbling down the nearby road. He caught sight of Luke and the other men near the edge of the woods and called out, "Have you seen General Beauregard in the area? I need to let him know that General Johnston's been shot."

"Where'd he get shot?" asked Luke.

"Near the peach orchard up ahead. Where he was leadin' an attack."

Luke knew the peach orchard he meant. He'd seen it in the morning sunlight, blooming defiantly in the midst of battle.

"No, I meant where's the wound?"

"In the leg, back of the knee, they say," replied the soldier, glad for a chance to stop and catch his breath for a moment.

"Think he'll be okay?" Luke asked.

"Dunno. Nobody knew he was wounded until he almost fainted on his horse."

"Couldn't they find any medics?"

"They say the general had sent 'em over to fix up some wounded Yankee prisoners. Can you believe that?"

"I hope it ain't serious."

"They'd got 'im off his horse and stretched him out last I saw of 'im." The soldier gave a quick wave. "Gotta go. I need to find General Beauregard, if you ain't seen 'im around here."

Luke packed up the dried beef he had left and decided to move toward the peach orchard, which wasn't far away. As he trudged up what he'd heard his captain call the Savannah Road, he came upon a gray-bearded man, sitting on a grassy bank, his head bowed and his hands hanging limp on his knees, his gun leaning against his shoulder.

"You all right, sir?" Luke asked.

"I'm fine, boy," he growled. Then, like an afterthought, he added in a gravelly whisper. "The general is dead."

"General Johnston?" Luke asked. "But I thought he jes' had a slight leg wound."

"Bled to death in his boot, they say. Nobody noticed till it was too late. They don't want us to know, but I seen it myself."

Luke sat down beside the man. His stomach felt queasy. The feeling was not unfamiliar. Throughout the morning he'd been nauseous. In fact, he'd thrown up once when he happened upon a body in the woods, belly split open to reveal its innards and its eyes wide with surprise.

"You look mighty young to be on a battlefield," the old man said.

"I'm thirteen." Luke squared his shoulders.

"Too durn young, I reckon," the man muttered and spat onto the road. He rose wearily to his feet, hoisted his rifle, and began to trudge with resignation toward a new sound of gunfire in the distance.

Luke followed him until he reached the place where General Johnston lay on the ground. In the distance, Luke could see the peach orchard where the battle had been fought and where pale pink petals had begun to fall from the trees, landing like decorations on the bodies of the dead men lying here and there.

Field officers were gathered around the general's body, some kneeling, with their heads bowed. One of them was standing to one side, holding the reins of Fire Eater, the horse the general had been riding that morning when he came to camp. The horse was stamping its foot.

Luke stood at a distance and took off his cap the way his mama had taught him when he ought to show respect. He watched as two litter-bearers came with a stretcher. They wrapped the general's body in a blanket to carry it, Luke presumed, to the nearest field wagon. All the surrounding officers stood at attention as they toted the litter away, and the man holding Fire Eater's reins followed the general's body, leading his horse. As they left the scene, one of the men, a major, raised his right hand, palm outward, to his cap in salute as the medics disappeared among the trees. The others followed suit. Once the moment of reverence for the fallen general passed, the officers stood together and talked in quiet tones.

What did it mean for the battle? Luke wondered. *Was it over? Had they won or lost?* It was hard to tell. To him it looked as though everyone had lost. So many dead men lay scattered through the fields and woods, some wearing blue, some gray or brown. Except for that, they all looked the same. Pale and lifeless. Hopeless. Gone.

The battle hadn't been at all like he'd supposed. He had imagined it filled with glory and drums and songs and bright-colored flags waving in the breeze, brave men in splendid uniform, carrying shiny rifles and swords and marching in step against a faceless, evil enemy they were sworn to defeat. In fact, the entire day had been nasty and ugly, filled instead with moans and hideous wounds, dead bodies crushing the blooming violets, and red blood oozing onto the tender spring grass. Some of the dead, like Jimmy, were still in their teens; others were old men who ought to be home teaching their grandsons how to fish.

It ain't right, Luke thought.

"Come on, boy," a red-headed Confederate limping down the road back toward the Landing beckoned to him. "Ain't no need to jes' stand there gapin'. They's a war to be fought." Luke propped his gun against his shoulder and fell into step behind the soldier. Blood stained the right leg of the man's trousers. *If he can keep goin' wounded, I guess I can keep goin' too,* Luke thought, lifting his chin and trying to remember how to be brave.

For the rest of the afternoon, when he shot at the enemy, he tried not to see their faces. He tried to imagine that they were rabbits or raccoons he was trying to kill for his family's supper. The commandment, always in his mother's voice, *Thou shalt not kill,* reverberated in his head. *Animals you eat don't count*, his daddy would always say. But he wouldn't ever let Luke kill animals for sport. When Luke left home, none of them thought he'd be carrying a gun and shooting at people. They thought he was only going to help out around camp, carry messages and such. His mama would be worried sick if she could see him now.

The fact is, Luke wasn't sure whether he'd killed anyone during the day's battle or not. He'd made an effort not to look after he shot. In spite of himself, he'd seen one man fall. But several other shots rang out simultaneous to his, and he didn't know whether he was the person to bring down the Union soldier or not. It was better not to know. Still, surely his daddy wouldn't mind him killing the enemy. Surely his daddy would be proud that he hadn't run away from the battle, that he'd shown courage. More than either one of them ever knew he had.

As he heard an explosion just ahead, Luke fell to the ground and covered his head, as he saw the other men do. The Union troops had gunboats stationed on the river, and they had been firing cannon shot off and on all day. It was probably best not to get too close to the river, Luke thought, but men seemed to be going in all directions around him, some slogging to the rear, others running toward the cannon fire, which seemed to be getting ever closer. They thought they had the Yankees trapped on the riverbank, but Luke wasn't so sure.

By the time the afternoon grew golden, Luke had run out of ammunition again. The men he'd been following all day marched on ahead, while he looked for new ammunition. As he was searching the leather satchel of yet another dead body for cartridges, he sensed someone standing nearby. He jerked his head around and saw a craggy-faced man in blue with a Springfield rifle aimed directly at him. The man's face froze at the sight of Luke.

The boy stood up hastily, his heart beating wildly. He jammed the stock of his gun against the ground, still fumbling with his other hand in the satchel for a cartridge. He knew time was against him. Some of the men could reload and fire three shots within a minute. Luke's experience was limited. It took him a lot longer. Especially with a gun pointed at him. His fingers closed around the paper cartridge. He ripped off the end with chattering teeth. His fingers trembled as he tried to pour the powder into the gun barrel. At any second he expected the man to fire. But to his surprise, the soldier lowered his weapon.

"I ain't here to kill boys," Luke heard him mutter as he turned his back and loped away toward the river. The boy was groping now for his ramrod to shove the minié ball down his gun barrel. The man got farther and farther away. He didn't look back.

Finally, after what seemed like hours, Luke raised his gun to his shoulder and tried to take aim, but his hands were still shaking. He could see the man weaving among the trees. His captain had told him to shoot anything in blue. But should that apply to a man who spared his life? Luke peered down the barrel of his gun, trying to get the man in his sights. A tree stood in the way, then another tree, then another. Luke aimed his gun first on one side of the trees, then on the other, waiting for a clear shot. It seemed impossible in this dense wood. And how could he shoot a man in the back? A man who could have killed him easily at such close range.

He heard his mama's voice again in his ear, *Thou shalt not kill.* It was a commandment from God. *Thou shalt not kill. Blessed are the merciful, for they shall obtain mercy.* The man had been merciful. Luke should be dead now, but here he was, his rifle braced against his shoulder, aiming toward the man who had spared his life.

None of it seemed to make any sense. The man had a hard face, but he didn't shoot. Why hadn't he fired? *He was merciful*, Luke thought. *And he shall obtain mercy.* He lowered his musket, and his legs seemed to give way as he sat down hard under a tree not far from the dead soldier. He put his face in his hands and felt hot tears spring to his eyes when he realized all of a sudden that he had wet himself.

The sun was getting lower in the sky now. When it began to sink below the horizon, General Beauregard called a halt to the attack. The soldiers in gray were puzzled, but relieved. Some of them thought the Yankees looked like they were on their last legs and that they could finish them off easily. Others weren't so sure. Union gunboats continued to shell the Confederate troops, now within range, as they pushed the Yankees closer to the river. General Beauregard also saw the danger, and he could see that his troops were tired. They had hardly eaten all day, and tonight they could make cookfires and have a decent hot meal. Besides, it was hard to fight in the dark when you couldn't see the enemy or tell a blue uniform from a gray one. They'd be fresher in the morning after a night's sleep, and he was hopeful that they could finish the job then.

Before he returned to camp, Luke wanted to find a pond or creek where he could rinse out his trousers. He had seen a small body of water a way back and made for the spot. But when he got there, he was horrified to see the bodies of dead men littering the banks and reeds of the pond. He wondered if they were dying men who had crawled there to get a drink or wash their wounds. He noticed that the water around the edges was the color of his daddy's pond in the winter, rusty with the bitter tannins of dead, fallen leaves. But Luke knew there were no dead leaves this time of year and that the reddish tint of the water was blood. With the now-familiar taste of bile in his throat, he turned away, trying not to vomit. Perhaps, he thought, his pants would dry before he reached camp. Perhaps he could rinse them with water from his canteen. Perhaps no one would notice. Perhaps. Thank God this day was coming to an end.

CHAPTER SIX

Ethan

April 6, 1862, Union Camp

Ethan had been awakened at dawn by the piercing yells of the advancing Confederates. He'd jumped up from his cot, thrown on his blue trousers, and rushed outside into the clear April morning.

The camp was in chaos. Tents nearest the woods were being ripped open by bayonets, their canvas flapping in the breeze. He could see little puffs of smoke from Confederate guns followed by loud pops of musket fire that echoed across the open field. Rebel troops were pouring relentlessly into the camp, startling birds to flight that, only moments before, had been pecking at the ground around the cook's tent looking for food. It was the hostile screams from the gaping mouths of the men in gray that terrified Ethan most, those Rebel yells, as the troops called them. They sounded like wild animals. He covered his ears. Then he thought, *My drum.* Perhaps he could drown them out with his drum.

He raced back inside the tent to fetch his jacket and kepi cap, grab his drum and drumsticks, and hustle out into the open once more. Trying not to flinch at the screams and gunfire, he planted himself beside his tent to beat the long roll, the men's call to arms. Though he had not been ordered to do so, he knew it was the only thing that made sense, the only thing that could defeat those yells.

Two tents away, another boy named Johnny Craig crawled out of his shelter as well, drum and drumsticks in hand, and began, like Ethan, to sound the long roll. Several other sleepy looking drummer boys did likewise. Theirs seemed to be the only military order in the camp, as they stood united, beating their drums and watching the horrors unfold around them.

Many of the men were already awake when the attack started—shaving, drinking coffee around the campfires, or eating their breakfast. Now they were scrambling to load their rifles, swinging their swords at the running Rebs, or lying already dead or wounded in the midst of the chaos. Ethan saw one fallen soldier sprawled outside a nearby tent, with shaving cream covering the lower half of his face like a white beard.

Once the Union troops recovered from the surprise of the

morning attack and were able to regroup, they did their best to hold back the Rebs, but the men in gray seemed to be everywhere, behind every tree or bush. Ethan followed the men in his unit as best he could. Tramping through the woods and fields among the troops, he tried to beat the cadence when they marched, but in spite of his efforts there was little sign of the even ranks and orderly attacks they drilled for back in camp. Without those, his drumbeats seemed superfluous.

Ethan tried to stay as close to General Wallace and his horse as he could to relay his commands by drumbeat. The general's shouted orders could not be heard very far through the sounds of gun and cannon fire. Even the drum rolls that signaled attack or retreat were difficult to hear above the noise, but Ethan did his best.

He caught up with the general and his men entrenched behind a thicket of tangled brush along a road beside what General Wallace called Duncan's cotton field. The fighting was fierce as the Confederates attacked again and again. There was little need for his drumming during the battles, and Ethan hunkered down behind a splintered tree as the bullets flew by, striking all around him.

"Like a durn hornet's nest in here," he heard one man mutter, commenting on the minié balls that whizzed by. Ethan agreed. He hadn't ever been so scared or felt so vulnerable. To make it worse, he felt useless. Finally, the general noticed him sitting there and ordered him back to a safer position behind the line.

The battle went on for hours, and Ethan wasn't sure what he should be doing now. The fighting along Duncan's farm road was not made up of the organized lines and orderly attacks the men had drilled for. From where he waited, the fight seemed to Ethan to consist mostly of soldiers on their own, trying not to be killed. He didn't have a gun, and he didn't really worry about getting shot, unless it was by accident, which had been a real possibility back where his unit was. But the general had assured all the drummer boys that soldiers would not deliberately shoot at them. Unarmed men like medics were also off limits to enemy soldiers. It was understood as one of the rules of civilized warfare.

Still, Ethan wanted to be useful, even if he didn't carry a gun. For a while he laid down his drum and followed the medics, helping to carry wounded soldiers off the battlefield and to the medical wagons, if they could get to them and if the medics thought their lives could be saved. But Ethan was too small to carry grown men for very long. After an exhausting two hours, he retrieved his drum and looked for a place he could safely rest for a moment or two. Up ahead, he spotted a small grove of trees that stood like an oasis in the middle of an empty field. He watched for a while for signs of military activity but saw no gunfire from the area and no evidence of troops—Union or Confederate. Cautiously, he approached and stepped into the shadow of the woods.

No one was there, only trees and a thick undergrowth of small bushes and brambles. As he walked on, wading through the vines that snatched at his feet, he discovered, at the very center of the grove, a small sunny glen that dropped a few feet to a dry creek bed below. There, except for the sounds of gunfire and cannon, which were only slightly muted by the trees and bushes, he could almost forget the war. The glen was empty of dead bodies and provided an unexpected respite from the mayhem about him. The warm sun shone down on his back as he sat down on the sloping ground and let the green beauty of early April wash over him. For a while he thought about nothing at all, just letting his body drink in the sunshine. But his conscience would not let him rest for long.

When he emerged to rejoin the other troops, he was aware that the numbers of the Union soldiers seemed to be diminishing. They were falling back farther and farther. Most of the men tried to stand their ground, but, outnumbered as they were, they were overwhelmed by the relentless assault of the Rebel troops. There seemed to be no escape. Finally, the officers ordered a retreat toward the river, where they sought safety for their men in the protection of the two gunboats, the *Tyler* and the *Lexington*, which lay in wait at Pittsburgh Landing.

Ethan retreated with the other men as they moved closer and closer to the river. Once it was safe for the gunboats to fire over their heads and not risk hitting their own troops, they began to shell the approaching Confederates more frequently in an effort to scatter them and drive them back. They didn't always hit their targets, but they hit them often enough to make the Rebs fall back a bit, trying to stay out of range.

Everyone was discouraged, but Ethan felt proud of the men he knew in his division, who had shown courage and fought hard all day. They'd held out longer than any of the other troops, a bearded man with a bandage on his head told him. But they had also lost many comrades, killed or wounded, he said.

"The general was one of those who got caught in the crossfire during our retreat," the man said. He was wounded, but I reckon he didn't know how bad it was.

By dusk, all of the men were so exhausted that many of them didn't seem to care whether they lived or died. They would plop down behind any tree that provided shelter, anywhere, just for a moment's rest. He knew how they felt.

All day long both officers and men had kept their eyes and hopes on the fast-flowing waters of the Tennessee, as they awaited the arrival of Buell's Army of the Ohio. A landing of fresh soldiers on the river's muddy banks could be their salvation. But no new boats arrived carrying reinforcements. The Union troops, who had been camped so leisurely near the Tennessee River just the day before, were fighting desperately for their very lives and trying to cling to the hope that any minute Buell's men might come to save them. But they were growing increasingly pessimistic. Their hopes were waning.

Their only other chance, some of the soldiers seemed to think, was to save themselves, even if they had to run away from the battlefield altogether and hide like cowards under the cover of distant woods or in the shallow caves along the steep river bank.

Ethan listened as the men talked among themselves, expressing a fear that once it was dark, the Rebs could sneak through the trees, and the troops manning the gunboats would never see them or know where they were. Everyone, both officers and men, expected darkness to bring a final Rebel assault, which would, they all feared, end the battle with a Confederate victory.

"Think Buell's men will get here before this danged war is over?" Ethan heard one man mutter, as he poured powder into his gun muzzle.

"Don't look like it," another replied, as he too was reloading his rifle. Ethan thought it must have been the thousandth time he had watched men load and reload throughout the day.

The Rebel assault seemed relentless. Despite his short rest, Ethan, like the other troops around him, was exhausted. The attack had begun before he woke up, and he hadn't had breakfast, except for a single biscuit he had grabbed as he was running by the cook's tent. He hadn't really thought about it until afternoon, with so much going on, but then his empty stomach began to rumble. He was hungry and ready to eat anything—even the hardtack he so despised.

As the sun began to set, the Union troops became even more

nervous, expecting any minute the final onslaught by the Rebs that would seal the end of the battle as a southern victory. They waited. But nothing happened.

As night came on, the Confederates surprised the Union officers by pulling back. An eerie quiet settled over the battlefield. The growing darkness was pierced only by the moans of dying men scattered throughout the fields and woods. The day that had begun with such savage horror was now oddly still.

Medics took advantage of the lull to go back to the battlefield for wounded men. Ethan followed them, realizing that he was wandering farther and farther from his own unit. He would try to find them later. Now, tired as he was, he still wanted to help. He kept remembering his father. He had seen his father fall and knew that he had been killed instantly. But if he had just been wounded, Ethan would have wanted the medics to come and try to save his life. The boy could imagine how awful it would be to be wounded and lying there, helpless, in the dark.

With caution, the medics moved toward an area where some of the worst fighting had taken place. They approached the peach orchard where a bloody skirmish had occurred earlier in the day and where, they said, one of the Rebel generals had died. Before the battle, the day before, Ethan remembered, it had been a beautiful sight, with blossoms still barely clinging to the trees. Beyond the orchard, tender sprouts of the newly planted cotton field—Widow Bell's Field, they called it—had peeked through the ground. But now the plowed earth was trampled and the small shoots smashed down by the boots of marching men. The blood of the dead and wounded had spilled into the furrows. The peach blossoms were falling like tears on the men who lay unmoving beneath the trees.

They reminded Ethan of snow, as they began to cover the ground in a rising breeze. Ethan wondered if there were enough petals, the light pink fading to a whitish-gray in the gathering dark, to bury all the bodies. He would never see the winter snows in his home state in quite the same way again. He watched around him, mesmerized, as medics quietly continued to gather the wounded one by one onto stretchers and carry them to wagons, already filled and waiting on the edge of the orchard. But there weren't enough medics or wagons to gather them all. Many would lie here, groaning throughout the night and through the coming storm that Ethan could smell already in the air.

He thought of the day his pa had fallen at Belmont, how he waited there with his body throughout the night until finally two men with a litter arrived to pick up his father's corpse to carry it back to camp to be identified. Recovering the lifeless bodies was always the last thing they did. He had marched alongside them, beating his drum slowly as tears rolled down his cheeks. Now he waited again, watching darkness creep over the field, the orchard, and the dead.

Once the medics gave up their chore for the night, Ethan wasn't sure how to find his company. The Confederates had swarmed over their former campsite and settled as squatters in the Union tents, so there was no returning to his original camp. He walked in darkness up the Savannah Road toward the river. Small clusters of troops were gathered here and there. He had no idea where he would spend the night. Nothing was as it should be. Following the road, he finally came across the remaining men from his unit, who had settled in an improvised camp for the night. Relieved to find them, Ethan shared in whatever food they had among them before he bedded down. He was too tired to sit around a campfire and commiserate with the others.

In spite of his fatigue, he still lay awake at midnight, listening to the hard rain pound on the canvas of the makeshift tent he was sharing now with Johnny Craig. Beside him was his drum, rolled up in oilcloth to keep it dry. He knew that, if the rain continued, the ground would be soaked. He thought of the little creek where he'd met Luke the day before the battle. By morning it would no doubt be swollen. Unless the sun came out early and burned hot enough to dry the ground, the army would slog around in the mud the next day.

He let his mind drift to the southern boy he'd met the day before—Luke—and wondered if he had heard the sounds of the battle from his daddy's farm. *He wasn't much different from me*, thought Ethan. It seemed odd that their people were on different sides in this war. Luke didn't seem like an enemy. *I could've beat him at arm wrestling if he hadn't cheated like that.* Ethan smiled in spite of himself at his own gullibility. *Maybe*, he thought. *Maybe next time I will.*

CHAPTER SEVEN

Luke

It was almost fully dark now, and there was no moon. Luke caught up with one of the young soldiers he knew, and together the two followed in the footsteps of some of the men from their company. As they tramped through the woods, Luke shuddered at the bodies sprawled here and there. He avoided them as best he could. They had all heard that their battalion was camping in relative ease in an abandoned Union camp. They could see the campfire glowing in the distance as they approached. It was a welcome sight. When they finally reached the camp, Luke sat down near the fire, his legs practically giving way with fatigue.

After a scant supper and a furtive effort to clean his pants with water from his refilled canteen, he undressed and fell wearily onto a cot in a tent much better than the one he had slept in the night before.

He was so exhausted that he expected to fall asleep at once. He did doze off, but a pounding rain on his tent's roof and the intermittent firing of Union gunboats, aimed at disturbing the Confederates' rest, woke him up and kept him awake much of the night. On one or two occasions when he did drop off to sleep, a sudden scream from the medical tent, where doctors were working to try to save the lives of the wounded men, jolted him awake again.

He could only imagine the horrors that went on in that tent. He had vomited again when he walked into the camp and saw the pile of bloody arms and legs in a ditch near the hospital tent. He'd never seen a dead man before that day, but today he'd seen enough to last him for all eternity. And maybe he'd even killed some of them.

Only the night before, Jimmy had been lying on a blanket next to him, snoring loudly. Luke had stuffed cotton in his ears to keep out the annoying sound. But he would eagerly trade the sounds he was hearing tonight for the welcome rumble of Jimmy's snores. This day, he knew, would haunt him for the rest of his life. And how could he ever tell Aunt Lucie what happened to her son? He heard the sound of crying coming from somewhere. Then he realized it was coming from inside his tent, from his own cot, from his own body.

He wiped his eyes with the tail of his undershirt and forced himself to think of something other than Jimmy's death. His mind conjured up the face of the Yankee boy from the day before—*Ethan*—and the peaceful creek where they'd met. He'd heard drumming during the morning attack and wondered if it was Ethan. But he hadn't heard it later in the day. *Is he still alive?* The question passed unbidden through Luke's mind.

Ethan still reminded Luke of Noah Willingham, only Noah couldn't wrestle nearly as good as Ethan. He wondered if Ethan could also shoot marbles better than Noah. He let the peace of his memories creep over him. And before he knew it, he was finally asleep and dreaming of his home and school in Georgia. Even the sound of Union cannon fire did not waken him. It blended with the thunder of the storm and was absorbed into his dreams.

CHAPTER EIGHT

Ethan

Ethan didn't sleep well at all—not at first. He was not used to sleeping on the bare ground when everything was wet and smelled of damp wool and mud. The sound of cannon fire from the gunboats on the river, which seemed to come every quarter hour throughout the night just as he was drifting off to sleep, didn't help. He knew it was meant to unnerve the Rebs, but it unnerved him too.

He waited for morning, dreading what would come. He'd felt almost useless throughout the day. It had become difficult, almost impossible, to keep up with the general or any other officers, all of whom were mounted on horseback. He thought of the small copse of trees with the sunny glen inside, which had provided a respite for him in the middle of the day. Maybe, when he needed to get away for a while, he could find it again tomorrow, unless the area was swarming with Rebs.

He was only vaguely aware, through the sound of the rain, of a scurry of activity at the landing. But his brain was too tired, and his mind so filled with the swirling memories and sounds of battle that he took in nothing else, except the cannon fire that kept him awake. Finally, only a few hours before dawn, the firing ceased, and he drifted into an uneasy sleep, hard and dreamless, unaware of the fevered preparations going on around him.

CHAPTER NINE

Luke

April 7, 1862

The rain passed before morning. The April sun was rising as the bugler in the Confederate camp sounded reveille. This time the Yankees knew they were coming. There was no more need for secrecy and quiet.

Luke climbed wearily from the cot and put his bare feet on the soggy earth where the rain had seeped in under the tent. His right shoulder was sore where the kick of the gunstock had left bruises. He rubbed it with the heel of his hand before he put on his shirt again. His pants were still damp in the crotch where he had poured water to clean them the night before, but he put them on anyway, despite their clammy feel. He didn't have another pair.

The camp cooks were busy tending their fires as Luke walked

toward the smells of a hot breakfast. He poured himself a cup of coffee, real coffee that had been found by the cooks among abandoned Union supplies. He wolfed down some boiled beef and a chunk of bread someone had put on one of the barrels the soldiers were using as a table. Anything tasted good this morning, he was so hungry. The men wasted little time breaking their fast because General Beauregard was eager to finish off the Union army.

But before they could get the units organized for a march, brazen Union soldiers, reinforced in number and spirit by the arrival during the night of General Buell's troops, were already attacking the camp. It was like an echo of the attack from the previous morning, only this time the situation was reversed.

"Fire! Fire!" a Confederate lieutenant Luke did not know shouted with impatience and a hint of panic in his voice. He sounded young. In fact, he was barely out of his teens and seemed determined to show his authority. It sounded as though the men were already firing as fast as they could load. The lieutenant echoed the captain's voice from the day before, "If it's dressed in blue, shoot it."

Luke dashed quickly back to his tent to get his ammunition box and the canteen he'd filled the night before, when he remembered how thirsty he'd been that afternoon. He also grabbed Jimmy's musket—now his—and loaded it before he left the safety of the tent to rush out into the melee. Men were running from the open campsite toward the greater protection of the woods on the opposite side of the camp. Luke followed them.

The morning was still cool and even cooler once he reached the shade of the trees. Many of the bodies from the day before still lay there. They'd been washed clean by the night's rain. Their faces were gray with the pallor of death. Some of them looked as though they were sleeping, but others had their eyes wide open, staring straight ahead at nothing.

Luke shuddered. Moving on, he searched for a good spot where he could watch for oncoming Union soldiers, but one where he was not surrounded by dead bodies. Finally he fixed on a small persimmon tree on the edge of the woods. Its branches forked at shoulder height. He would be able to rest his gun in its junction and even swivel it to get the Yankees in his sights.

He propped his gun in the fork of the tree and waited.

He jumped when he heard a weak voice behind him say, "Water … Can you spare a drop of water?'

Luke turned to see where the voice came from. Behind a budding but scrubby elderberry bush, he caught sight of a pair of feet extended from blue trousers. They were unmoving. Luke hadn't noticed them before, but even if he had, he would have assumed they were the feet of a dead man. He peered cautiously around the bush. A Union soldier with a gaping head wound lay there, his head and shoulders propped against a hickory tree. His arms and hands stretched useless beside him, and his whole body seemed paralyzed, except for his eyes and mouth. He was a man in his late forties, maybe even fifty, and his beard was turning gray.

From under heavy lids, he fixed his eyes on Luke. His lips barely moved when he spoke. "Water ... please, a sip of water."

Instinctively Luke knelt beside him, unbuckled his canteen, and held it to the man's lips. *I was hungry and you gave Me food; I was thirsty and you gave Me drink.*

"Thank ye, boy. God bless," said the man after he had taken a drink. With his free hand, Luke wiped away the water that spilled down the man's chin.

"What the heck d'you think you're doin'?" The sharp voice cut through the morning air like a knife. "That there's a Yankee."

Luke turned to see the young lieutenant from the camp, mounted now on horseback.

"I was just ...," Luke began.

"I was just ...," the lieutenant mocked his words. "I was just ... nothin'," he spat out the words. "Shoot the devil."

"But I ... I think he's already dyin'," said Luke.

"I said, shoot him."

The Union soldier spoke quietly once again, his eyes fixed on Luke, "Thank ye, boy."

At that moment, the lieutenant, his eyes flashing and an impatient snarl on his lips, took out his pistol and shot the man in the chest. The wounded man groaned once and exhaled a deep breath. His lips turned up in what seemed almost a smile. Then his mouth fell open, his head dropped gently sideways toward his shoulder, and he was still.

Luke looked from the soldier to the lieutenant. "He was dyin' anyway, sir. I was just tryin' to ease his sufferin' a little, is all."

The lieutenant snorted in disgust. "I want 'em all to suffer. Th' only good Yankee's a dead Yankee. You 'member that, boy. And don't let me catch you wastin' water like that again. Y' hear?"

He wheeled his horse around in a tight circle and trotted away.

"Yes sir," Luke whispered to his disappearing back.

But he didn't mean it. The heart for battle had gone out of him. He looked down at the dead man for a long moment. *That could've been my daddy*, he thought. *Or Ethan's daddy. The only difference would've been the color of the uniform.*

He turned away and walked slowly into the deeper woods, where all the colors blended in the darker shade.

The battle raged on throughout the day, only this time, it was the Confederate troops that were being pushed back. More Union soldiers than Luke had ever seen before swarmed the open fields.

"We should've finished 'em off last night," he heard a man mutter.

"Where the dickens are they comin' from?" another said.

"Reinforcements, I reckon … Should've finished 'em off last

night," the man repeated, shaking his head.

Luke did his best to keep his gun loaded and tried to fire at the enemy. But he kept letting his eyes rise to their faces, and even though they were far away, he kept seeing the faces of his friends and family at the end of his gun sights. He knew he missed his mark.

CHAPTER TEN

Ethan

April 7, 1862

During the night, steamboats carrying General Buell's men had arrived in waves. They were greeted with enthusiasm by General Grant's weary troops, and throughout the night, officers had met and planned a new strategy of attack for the next day. All morning long, Ethan followed the troops, beating his drum whenever it was needed. As the men lined up to move forward, he was ready with the long roll, just as he had been ready to beat retreat the day before. But everything was happening so quickly that there was little time for very many of the orderly beats and marches he was trained for. Today Ethan was assigned to Colonel Tuttle, who had taken over command of the Second Division from General Wallace. The general had been wounded when his men were forced to retreat in a crossfire following a fierce battle to hold off the Confederates the day before. Rumor had it that he was near death. Otherwise, the main difference was that this time they were marching toward the enemy, not away.

Before long, the colonel galloped off, leaving Ethan, once more unsure about what he should do in the confusion of battle. He thought of helping the medics again, for they were always so busy.

He knew he could probably help more if he abandoned his drum for good and assisted the medics, who moved from here to there, carrying the wounded to waiting wagons. But he could never abandon his drum. Not for good. He would lay it down now and then on the same piece of oilskin he had wrapped it in the night before and which he kept in his haversack to keep out the damp. He never used the oilskin for himself. It was always for his drum. Even so he worried about it. Each time he came back to retrieve it, he would run his fingers over the varnished rim to make certain everything was intact.

He never wanted to lose his drum. He was especially proud of it because his pa had selected it for him when the two of them first went off to join the Illinois 7th. It was made by Horstmann Brothers, who, his pa said, made the best drums of all. Its body was rosewood, and its rims polished mahogany. It had a dark blue background with a hand-painted eagle and a flag shield for decoration. Ethan thought it the finest drum he had ever seen. It made him feel closer to his father when he could wake up every morning and see it perched on a campstool beside his cot. The night before, however, he'd had no cot or campstool. He'd slept on the damp ground, while his drum was safely wrapped in oilskin. Selecting that drum was the last thing he and his father had done together, except for marching into battle.

The fields and woods, as far as he could see, were still strewn with the dead and the wounded. Even carrying his drum, he could help the medics by checking the bodies to see which ones were still alive. Most of the time he had to touch them to feel a pulse or hold his hand in front of their faces to see if there was breath. Sometimes he could tell by the rise and fall of their chests. Or by their stillness. But sometimes the breath was so shallow that he couldn't be sure and had to check in other ways. It was a gut-wrenching job because every dead body made him think of his father, how he had lain there on the ground with a cannon ball through his chest. He thought his pa's face reflected the pain and surprise of being struck. But the medics told Ethan that he couldn't have suffered much because his death would have been immediate. Nobody could take a blow like that and live, they said. That was some consolation.

Ethan had gone home on the train to accompany his pa's body, and his ma had begged him to stay. But he felt it was his duty to go back. Besides, he had signed up for three years just like his pa had. He had no choice but to return. He and his pa had volunteered for the same company and thought they would be together throughout the war. Ethan had not realized what it would be like there without someone to check on him every morning and encourage him when he got tired or homesick. He was more homesick now than he ever thought possible, but he knew he had to bear it. None of the other drummer boys had fathers in the camp. *If they could do it*, he thought, *he could too.*

The afternoon before, by the flowing creek with the boy Luke, had made Ethan feel like he was back home, playing with a friend. Luke had made him briefly forget about the war. *We won't be able to get together at the creek like we'd planned*, he thought. He was pretty sure with all the fighting going on that Luke wouldn't be allowed to go anywhere, and he wondered what Luke would be doing now. Sitting in his mama's kitchen watching her make an apple pie maybe? Or reading a book? He smiled grimly as he thought of Luke's words, that they could meet again, "God willin' and the creek don't rise." With last night's rain, the creek had definitely risen.

"Have you checked that field over there, boy?" yelled a medic. Their wagon was already full of the wounded, but there would always be more.

"No sir, not yet," Ethan answered and started walking toward the very same cotton field he had passed through the afternoon before, where the neat furrows and young plants were trampled. But puddles of water now stood in the low places, mixing with the blood that seeped into the earth. As he walked among the bodies that lay in the field, mud clung to his shoes up to the laces. He found no one alive.

73

Suddenly he realized that he was all alone among the dead. The medics had disappeared with their wagon full of wounded men, hauling them back to a surgical tent. They would come back, he knew, but what was he to do in the meantime? He didn't want to wait out in the open, for fear someone might mistake him for a soldier.

Not far away, he knew, stood the little grove of trees he had come across the day before. Perhaps he could wait there until the medics returned. The sky had cleared, and the sun had come out. It would be good to spend a little time by himself, and he remembered the sunny hollow in the center of the small shaded wood. It seemed to draw him.

Just like the day before, it was empty of bodies, empty of soldiers. It was like a sanctuary in the midst of the war. There were not even any trees that had been splintered by cannon balls, like there were in the larger woods. His heart needed a rest as much as his body did. He found a spot under a tree that overlooked the dry creek bed of the day before. Now water stood at the bottom like a little pond, its banks covered with small yellow and white flowers whose names he did not know. He sat down and pulled some leaves off a nearby shrub to try to clean some of the mud off his boots.

He could still hear the sounds of the war, but they seemed distant, and his mind managed to block them out. There were no birds trilling in the trees, and any squirrels who may have been there had hidden themselves completely inside hollows in the tree trunks, seeking, like him, a place of peace.

CHAPTER ELEVEN

Luke / Ethan

Luke held his musket high to keep it from tangling in the brambles as he walked into the shelter of a small stand of trees in the middle of the big field. From there, he thought, he could see the enemy, but they couldn't see him. And neither could the young lieutenant, who had dogged him throughout the morning. It was well past dinnertime, and he was hungry, longing for a hot meal he knew he'd not get anytime soon. All he'd had to eat was the ham biscuit he'd grabbed as he fled the early morning attackers.

The sun, still high in the sky, was shut out of all but the center of this glen. It was only a small copse of hardwoods with a sunny center that sloped down to a ditch filled with standing water from last night's rain. The banks were covered with small yellow flowers he thought he'd heard his mama call buttercups and, nearer the bottom, with the tiny white blooms of watercress. The little grove looked out of place in this vast empty plain, a place of peace, different from the rest. He wanted to stop here, put down his gun, lean against a tree trunk, and take a rest, though he dared not falter long in his move toward the Yankee line.

The young lieutenant who'd ordered him to shoot the dying man had kept an eye on him throughout the morning, as though he expected him to repeat his military sin of giving a drink to the enemy. Luke was trying to stay out of his line of sight, and with that in mind, he had decided to duck for a brief respite into the little stand of woods.

What was so different, he wondered, as he relived the incident in his mind, between his small act of kindness and the general sending his medics to tend the wounded Union captives, while he himself bled to death? There wasn't much about this war Luke understood. Except that he was supposed to kill people he didn't even know. Except that some people acted one way and some another. It made no sense at all to him. Were there rules in war against treating wounded people, who were no harm to anybody anymore, the way you'd want to be treated? If so, why hadn't the general followed them? Was the Golden Rule supposed to end on the edge of the battlefield?

The preacher at the little Presbyterian church where his family attended services back home always preached "Love your enemies," at least until this war started. He didn't exactly backtrack, but he hadn't used that scripture about turning the other cheek or even that story about the good Samaritan for any of his sermons after the war fever got so hot in Waycross. *Had God changed His mind? And whose side was God on anyhow? Why did He let Jimmy get killed?* It was like a big puzzle that Luke had put together wrong or didn't have all the pieces to. He just needed time to think. Maybe he would take a moment or two here in the shelter of the woods to rest for a few minutes and let his body and his mind relax.

Suddenly he saw a flicker of movement on the other side of the little hollow, a flash of blue behind a thick bush that caught his eye. He raised his loaded gun to his shoulder now almost by instinct, but he didn't want to pull the trigger.

"Come on out, Yank," he called. "I know you're there. I see you, so you might as well come out in the open." Maybe he could take this one prisoner. Maybe he wouldn't have to shoot after all.

The shape behind the bush didn't move.

"What's the matter? You chicken?" Luke called out, keeping his gun pointed toward the bush.

"Ain't scared of you, Reb," a defiant voice answered.

A familiar figure stood up and stepped cautiously from behind the bush and into the sunlight. It was Ethan—his drum dangling from his neck, drumsticks in his hands. His eyes were wide with fear, and his body was tense.

In spite of himself, Luke felt a grin break across his face as he lowered his gun. "Hey ... Ethan," he called. "Is that you?"

Ethan's fear gave way to puzzlement. Then, recognizing Luke, his body relaxed. He shook his head in disbelief, and a slow smile spread across his face. He raised an arm to wave and opened his mouth to say something.

But before he could utter a word, a shot rang out. Ethan's eyes, fixed on Luke, seemed to widen with disbelief. His smile faded, and he dropped to his knees.

Then another shot. The impact against the boy's body knocked him backward, his knees bent to one side. He lay there unmoving, the sun bathing his face with light. Luke stared at him, stunned.

The young lieutenant who had been watching Luke throughout the day rode into the clearing on his horse.

"What in tarnation are you gapin' at, boy? Why didn't *you* shoot him?"

"He ... He wasn't armed, sir," Luke stammered. "And he was my friend."

"Your what?" The lieutenant laughed an ugly laugh. "Your friend, your little friend," he mocked Luke. "He was a Yankee, you fool. He wasn't nobody's friend."

The horse stamped his foot on the soft earth. "You know, you're about as useful as a cockroach in this here war. I got my eye on you, boy. I been followin' you, and I don't like what I see. You mess up again, and I'll see you hanged for treason."

The horse stamped again, and the lieutenant pulled back on the rein at the same time he slapped the horse's withers. The animal reared in confusion and whinnied. Then the lieutenant gave him his head, allowing him to dart out through the copse of trees and into the sunlight on the other side. In the distance a cannon roared. The lieutenant turned his horse toward the sound of cannon fire and galloped away.

Luke stood in silence, numb with disbelief, staring at Ethan's body lying so still among the blossoms on the hollow's edge. He tried to make sense of it all, but his mind was a jumble. Ethan lay there like he was sleeping, except for his eyes, which were still open as though gazing straight into the sunlight. His drum had rolled to one side. His arm was still raised in eternal greeting. His hand, palm upward, fingers slightly curled, still held one of the drumsticks. The other had slipped from his hand and lay on the ground beside him.

Luke could not move. His heart pounded in his chest as he gazed at Ethan's uncomprehending face. He was what Luke's mama would have called a handsome boy. His eyes were dark blue, except for the fixed black pupils, and his dark hair needed cutting. Luke wondered if Ethan's mother cut his hair. It looked like it hadn't been cut for a long time. His locks, held in place by the kepi cap still jammed on Ethan's head, hung in soft waves below his ears. It was a dumb thing to wonder about, Luke knew, but it kept him from having to absorb the truth of what had happened.

A cannon fired again. The noise startled Luke into action. He crossed the little hollow to where Ethan lay and sat down beside his still form. He didn't care what the lieutenant said. They could hang him for all he cared. But he couldn't leave his friend there alone. He couldn't just walk away.

With tentative fingers, Luke leaned over Ethan's body to close his eyes and touch his cheek. He had never touched a dead person before, not their skin anyhow. Even when he'd rummaged about dead bodies for ammunition, he was careful not to touch a dead hand or face, as though death might rub off on him. But Ethan's face was warm, just like he was still alive. Now, with his eyes closed, he looked more peaceful, as though he were taking a nap. Luke looked at him intently, unable to tear his eyes away, but he felt too numb to cry, like he had already used up all his tears.

"I'm real sorry, Ethan," he said. "I speck we would've been good friends, things bein' different. You could've beat me at arm wrestlin' if I hadn't tricked you. Fact is, that's why I did it … 'cause I could tell you was real strong. I prob'ly couldn't have beat you any other way."

Musket fire was growing closer. Luke couldn't tell if the sounds came from Union guns or Confederate guns or both. Both probably. He didn't care. Luke looked at his own gun, Jimmy's gun, which was loaded with his last shot of ammunition. He picked it up. It felt cold and strange in his hands. He pointed the muzzle at the sky and fired it straight up in the air.

"I ain't got no more shot, Ethan. And I ain't gettin' no more. I can't kill nobody else." He still wasn't sure whether he had killed anybody or not, and he didn't want to know. His daddy always said he was a pretty good shot when they hunted together, but sometimes he missed. That was a comforting thought. But he knew one thing—he would never point his gun at another human being again—not as long as he lived.

"I bet you could play that drum real good," Luke said to Ethan's still form. "I bet your daddy, I mean your pa, was real proud of you." Luke thought about that for a while, and then he said out loud, "Maybe you're with your pa now. Your mama will be real sad, but I bet your pa is right glad to see you again." It was what he had been taught to believe, that when you die, you are reunited with all those folks who died before. He hoped it was true and that Ethan was with his daddy up in Heaven.

What could he do? It didn't seem right just to leave Ethan there alone. It didn't seem right to go back to the war and abandon his friend. He knew he couldn't stay here forever, but he felt called upon to do something.

Luke had no idea how long he sat beside Ethan's body, thinking about what would be a fitting tribute to his friend. Finally he took his shooter agate out of his pocket. It was his favorite marble and always won the games for him. He had brought it along for luck. But now, he reckoned, Ethan needed it more than he did. He warmed it in his hand for a moment and then put it in Ethan's pocket.

"You keep this for me," he said. "And when I get up to Heaven, maybe we can have a game."

Ethan lay still as an ant crawled across his face. Luke flicked it away, wishing he could find some of the medics that picked up the dead and wounded. He didn't want to leave Ethan alone in this hollow. He might never be found. But one thing he knew he had to do before he left that copse of trees.

The earth was soft and damp. He didn't have a shovel, but he did the best he could to dig with his hands. And when the ground got too hard underneath the top layer softened by the rain, he took out his pocket knife and kept on chipping away at the stubborn earth. When his hole was long enough and wide enough, he picked up Jimmy's gun from the ground and laid it in the hole. Then he covered it with dirt and leaves. He couldn't dig a hole deep enough to bury Ethan, and he hoped the seekers would find his body and send it home to his mama. But he buried Jimmy's musket there beside Ethan.

"This gun ain't never gonna hurt nobody else, Ethan. And I ain't gonna hurt nobody neither. I wish you'd a told me your mama's name so I could write her a letter and tell her we met. I'd tell her you were mighty brave. I'd tell her you could arm wrestle like a man. I'd tell her that we would have been friends … heck, that we *were* friends. And that I'm real sorry about what happened."

Then Luke stood up and took his hat in his hands. He bowed

his head and stood silent for a moment, brushing his eyes with the back of his hand. He wished he could remember all the words to the Twenty-third Psalm that his mama had tried to make him learn when he was ten, but he said it the best he could:

The Lord is my shepherd. He leadeth me beside still waters and maketh me lie down in green pastures. He restoreth my soul. And I will dwell in the house of the Lord forever. Amen.

It was the best he could do. He wasn't sure about the *Amen*, but it seemed right to say it.

Luke knelt once more beside Ethan's body and adjusted the kepi cap on his still head so that it would shield his closed eyes from the sun. Then he stood up again, gazing for one last time at his friend's body and worrying that those who gathered the dead from the battlefield might never find him here. They might never think to look in this little grove that seemed so untouched by war. He considered how he might help.

He bent down to pick up both the drumstick Ethan still held loosely in his hand as well as the one lying beside him on the ground. Walking to the edge of the shady grove into the afternoon sunlight, he laid the drumsticks side by side in a V-shape with the tips pointing like an arrow toward the grove. Perhaps the medics would see the drumsticks and understand his signal. He hoped so.

Luke could still hear the sounds of war in the distance, though they seemed quieter than before. He couldn't tell who was winning and who was losing. But he knew one thing for sure. For him this war was over. And he would never fight another.

He didn't know what they were fighting about anyway. Not really. Jimmy had said it was for the honor of the South and the southern way of life, whatever that was. Ethan had seemed to think it was about the slaves. Maybe it was both. But what did one have to do with the other? Was Uncle John a slave? Luke didn't even know whether his family owned him or just let him live on the farm and help out. But if they did own him, it wasn't right. He couldn't imagine the farm without Uncle John, but maybe he'd like to go find his lost son. And if he would, then he ought to be able to do it. If all this fighting was about trying to keep Uncle John a slave, then it was wrong. In fact, come to think of it, almost everything about this war seemed wrong.

The afternoon sun was getting lower to his right, and he judged that to be the west. Straight in front of him then must be south. That way and a little more to the east must be the way back to Georgia. If he headed that direction, he was bound to find a road sooner or later. Or maybe another train that would take him part of the way. He knew he still had another hard task in front of him. He had to tell Aunt Lucie what happened to Jimmy. He hoped she wouldn't be mad at him for not bringing home the gun.

The way back wouldn't be easy, he knew, but he was a man now, and he had to face up to a man's duties. And if Uncle John ever left, then Luke knew he would be needed on the farm. The way home was long, and it might take him several weeks. He could no longer depend on Jimmy to show him the way. He would have to find it for himself.

With that in mind, he put on his hat, secured his haversack on his back, and turned his footsteps toward home.

EPILOGUE

October 7, 1887, Shiloh Cemetery

"Do you reckon we'll ever find it, Daddy?" the boy asked, as he rambled among the tombstones. There were so many of them.

"All we can do is keep on tryin', son. I know he was from Illinois."

"What was his last name again?"

"Garner," his father said. He had made a trip to Springfield the month before to try to find out the full name of his friend, the drummer boy Ethan, and to make sure he hadn't been buried in Illinois. He had found out the name from a document in the courthouse that listed all the soldiers of the 7th Illinois. Once he found his name, he had looked for Ethan's mother and sisters, but all he learned was that after the war they'd moved away. No one seemed to know where. He scoured the cemeteries, but found no trace of Ethan's grave in Springfield.

His brief friendship with Ethan had been on Luke's mind for twenty-five years now, and he had to know the end of his story. Had the searchers found his body or not? Now that Luke worked for the railroad, it was easier to travel, and this was a trip he had wanted to make for a long time—back to the battlefield where it all happened—to find out for himself.

He had never forgotten the afternoon they had spent together by Owl Creek. He still remembered the drummer boy's friendly smile when they saw each other on the battlefield and before the bullet struck. And he could not wipe from his mind or his dreams Ethan's wide-eyed look of surprise and hurt, as he realized he'd been shot and fell backward in the hollow, his hand still raised in greeting. Luke had always hoped that Ethan never thought he was the person who held the gun.

"Tell me more about him, Daddy. Why was he so special to you?" Luke had told his son the story several times before, and he wanted to come along when his father decided to make this trip.

"I don't really know. He was a drummer boy from Illinois, just a year or two older than you. He was a good kid, and he didn't deserve to die."

"Is he why you named me Ethan?"

"Well, partly I reckon. I've never been able to forget him. It could've been me lying on that ground. In fact, once, it nearly was."

"What do you mean? What happened, Daddy?"

"A Yankee soldier had me in his gun sights, but he refused to shoot. He saw I was just a boy, and he lowered his gun."

"Were you carrying a gun?"

"I was. My cousin Jimmy's rifle, but that man didn't see me as an enemy."

"Why did the lieutenant shoot Ethan?"

"I don't know for sure, son. Ethan wasn't armed, and it was pretty generally understood that soldiers didn't shoot at drummer boys or medics, but I think it was really me the lieutenant wanted to shoot."

"What do you mean?"

"It was me he was mad at—not Ethan. And I think Ethan was just my substitute."

"Why did he want to shoot you?"

"I gave some water to a dyin' Yankee soldier."

"Was that a bad thing?

"I didn't think so, but it infuriated the lieutenant."

"I don't understand why it made him shoot Ethan."

"Well, sometimes even grownups get upset and take things out on people who didn't do 'em any wrong. Do you remember the time Johnny Taylor got mad at the teacher and went home and hit his little brother? Well, it was something like that. He couldn't hit the teacher, so he took out his anger against his brother instead. I think it was like that with the lieutenant. He couldn't shoot a soldier in his own army, even though I was the one who made him mad."

The boy thought for a moment. Then he asked, "Are you sorry we didn't win that war, Daddy?" Luke didn't say anything for a while, as he studied the Union tombstones in Shiloh Cemetery.

"You know, son, I think, in a way, we did win the war, though most people down South don't agree."

Young Ethan looked puzzled, "What do you mean?"

"Well, just think about it, if the South had won, you wouldn't be an American now."

"Gosh, I never thought of that."

"And I think it's a whole lot better that people like my old friend, Uncle John—I've told you about him—aren't slaves anymore. He's gone now, but at the end of his life, he was able to see his son again. His name was Walter. He'd been sold over in Alabama, but when freedom came, he left Alabama and came back to our farm to look for his daddy. I never saw Uncle John so happy in all my life. You know Walter Freeman and his boy Jeremiah, don't you? The people who sharecrop for Mr. Phillips? Well, Jeremiah is Uncle John's grandson. He lived long enough to see his son Walter again and even his grandson. I think he died a right happy man."

"There's a boy in my class at school, Furman Hicks, who hates the Yankees. He says they killed his grandpa and burned down his house near Macon."

"I know the Yankees did some mighty bad things in Georgia, Ethan. But I know for a fact they weren't all bad. Remember the one who wouldn't shoot me. Well, I think he must have been a good man, and I hope he made it home safe. War sometimes causes men to do things they would never do otherwise. People on both sides did some bad things."

"Did you kill anybody, Daddy?"

"I don't know, son, but I hope not. And I hope you never do either. I hope you never have to fight in a war."

The two fell silent as they roamed among the tombstones. Farther away a section with small stones marked the graves of unknown soldiers, but Luke and his son were exploring the section with taller stones, where the names were indicated. If Ethan's body had been found, surely someone would have been able to identify the drummer boy, Luke thought.

He watched the maple leaves drifting down around him in the Union cemetery. They reminded him of the peach blossoms that had fallen on the dead so many years ago. He smelled the brisk autumn air and felt somehow anxious. What if they didn't find the grave? What if he never knew? There were so many stones, so many dead from that awful two-day battle. From later reports after he had made it back home, he learned that the same afternoon he started his trek back to Georgia, the Confederates began their retreat back to Corinth, leaving behind a devastated landscape and many Confederate dead, Jimmy among them, now buried in mass graves somewhere on the battlefield. Only Union troops lay here beneath these neat rows of stones. Luke wished he could visit Jimmy's grave as well, but the mass graves, which held so many bodies, bore no names.

They searched on, taking alternate rows to look at all the stones, young Ethan moving more quickly than his father. The graves seemed endless.

Finally, as the afternoon was waning and the shadows of the gravestones were growing longer, the boy called from three rows away, "Here it is, Daddy. I found it."

Sure enough, as Luke approached, hat in his hand, he saw it—the white granite stone bearing the shape of a shield with a number at the top, the name Ethan Garner, curved beneath it like a rainbow, and in the middle, his home state, Illinois. Luke felt his heart pounding as he knelt down beside the stone and ran his fingers over the raised letters of Ethan's name.

"Thank God they found him," he said softly. He was silent for a long time, remembering. Then he asked, "Did you bring it, son?"

The boy nodded gravely.

"Are you sure you want to part with it? It's your favorite," his father said.

He nodded again, digging in his pockets for his polished agate marble. Then he knelt down beside his father and pressed it into the soft earth at the foot of the stone.

Luke could see his son's lips moving, but he made no sound. Young Ethan was praying over the gift he'd brought to his father's friend. Luke smiled and rested his hand on his son's shoulder.

The boy looked up. "Now when you get to Heaven, you can both have a good shooter and a real game."

"Thank you, son," his father said, tears springing to his eyes. Then, resting his hand on the top of the tombstone, he bid a final farewell to Ethan, the drummer boy. "Rest in peace, my friend."

Luke took a deep breath of the cool autumn air, glad to be alive in this stretch of green. Just for a moment, the terrible vision of the last time he saw this field, strewn with bodies of the dead and wounded, flitted through his mind. He quickly brushed it away, replacing it with a new memory of this now-peaceful spot, so different from the last time he was here. The land had healed, and there were no longer any signs of battle, except for an occasional scar on a tree, which, Luke knew, must have been struck by cannon fire or a minié ball. It felt right that it should finally be so quiet here, the air brisk and the leaves already burnished with red and gold, but the grass still green and living, a fitting memorial to all that had happened here.

The sun was starting to set, streaking the sky with red, as the pair rose and walked, hand in hand, through the long shadows of the marked graves, back toward the wagon that had brought them.

AUTHOR'S NOTE

It is ironic that *Shiloh*, a Hebrew word, means *peace*. In the history of the Civil War, however, it is remembered in terms of casualties as the most costly battle that had been fought up until that time in the history of America. Two of the bloodiest parts of the battle were those at the peach orchard, where General Johnston died, and at what would later come to be known as the Hornet's Nest, where General Wallace fell.

The Battle of Shiloh was over by mid-afternoon on April 7, when the Confederate troops accepted defeat and began their retreat back to Corinth, Mississippi, which would be the site of two later battles in 1862.

Luke, who had never officially mustered in, did not go with them. By the time, General Beauregard ordered a retreat, Luke was already leaving the battlefield to begin his long voyage home. He would reach his home near Waycross, Georgia, twelve days later, where he grew up to have a family of his own. He moved to nearby

Cochran, Georgia, where he worked for the East Tennessee, Virginia, and Georgia Railroad.

The State of Tennessee, where Shiloh battlefield is located, was the last southern state to secede from the Union. It was also one of the most divided states in terms of its support for the Union and the Confederacy. People from East Tennessee, few of whom owned slaves, tended to side with the Union, while those in Middle and West Tennessee, where slave owners were more prevalent, tended to sympathize with the Confederacy. More battles were fought in Tennessee than in any other state except Virginia.

The Boys of Shiloh is my first effort at writing a book for young readers. Although I have previously published eleven books for adults—eight nonfiction works, two historical fiction novels, and one book of poetry, this is a new undertaking for me. This book is the result of a trip my late husband and I took with my grandson, Gabe, to the battlefield at Shiloh, Tennessee, when he was about twelve years old. By the time this book goes to press, he will be in college. Thanks for the inspiration, Gabe.

Both Luke and Ethan are fictional characters. The generals mentioned in the story and the battles they fought are real. I would like to thank my grandson, Luke, and his cousin, Ethan, for letting me use their names for the boys in my book. My young friend, Tristan, who was in the seventh grade when he read the first chapter of this book, was the one who kept urging me to finish the story and who was my first reader. I thank him for his encouragement and helpful feedback. It was he and his father, Brent, who suggested the epilogue.

I would also like to thank the following: Jill Reifschneider, a fifth-grade teacher (and my daughter-in-law), and Terina Black, parent volunteer and children's librarian, for allowing fifth-grade students at the Community School in Lake Washington School District in King County, Washington, to read and comment on the manuscript as one of their Literary Circle activities. I am especially grateful to A. J., Ben, Carmen, Chance, Elora, Lizzy, Nicole, Nolan, Olivia, and Townsend for their very helpful suggestions. In addition, I am grateful for the useful review of my young Virginia friend, Claire, who let me read to her class during a visit. As a result of all their comments, I have added a glossary to the text, changed the vocabulary in certain places, added more chapters from Ethan's point of view, and clarified some of the questions that arose, especially in the first chapter. I was very impressed with the insightful observations by these bright, young readers. Thank you all for your careful reading and great ideas.

Others who have commented on the book and helped with details in the manuscript include professor emerita Margaret Ordoubadian, a specialist in children's literature, historian Dr. Derek Frisby of Middle Tennessee State University's History Department, who read the manuscript for historical accuracy, Charles Spearman, park ranger at Shiloh Battlefield, who provided assistance with the battlefield map, and Kasey Johnson from the Georgia State Railroad

Museum in Savannah, Georgia, who set me straight on the route Luke and Jimmy would have taken to reach Corinth, Mississippi. And, finally, to my editor, Michelle Adkerson, and my designer, Art Growden, my sincere appreciation for all your good work.

I hope that the finished book will live up to their expectations.

GLOSSARY

agate – a hard, variegated stone, used in Germany from the mid-1800s to make marbles, which were imported to America, where marbles were not made until the late 19th century

banshee – a fairy from ancient Irish folklore, whose wailing was considered a forewarning of death

bile – a bitter-tasting yellowish liquid produced by the liver

brazen – bold, unashamed

brogan – a heavy, sturdy, work shoe that fits high around the ankle

canteen – a water container used by soldiers

captain – a military rank just above lieutenant but below major

chicory – a thick-rooted herb that can be ground up to make coffee. In the Civil War, cooks who didn't always have coffee beans made coffee from such substitutes as ground chicory, beets, rye, and acorns.

copse – a small group of trees; thicket; grove

corporal – a relatively low military rank, higher than private, but below sergeant

eddy – a circular movement of water; a small whirlpool

general – the highest army military rank, when used as a noun

gunstock– the stock or handle, usually of wood, to which the barrel of a gun is attached and by which one holds a gun. It rests against the shoulder and can "kick" (or recoil) when the gun is fired.

hardtack – a hard, dry biscuit made without salt but with only flour and water

haversack – a bag, usually made of canvas or leather, that carries a soldier's daily rations and necessities. It has a flap and a long strap that can be slung over the shoulder.

kepi cap – a military cap with a round flat top usually sloping toward the front and a visor or small bill (like the caps of the boys on the book cover)

lieutenant – the lowest rank for a commissioned officer in the army

major – a military rank above captain but below colonel

minié ball – a rifle or musket bullet, shaped like a cone, used during the 19th century

noncommittally (adv.) – describes an action or statement that does not express or reveal a decision toward a definite opinion or course of action

prattle – foolish or inconsequential talk

ramrod – a rod used to ram (or push) the charge of a muzzle-loading firearm down the barrel

Rebel – nickname given by Union troops to Confederate troops; a person in rebellion

Reb – a common abbreviation for *Rebel* used by Union troops during the Civil War

Rebel yell – a long, high-pitched yell that Confederate soldiers used to scare the enemy

reiterate – to repeat something you have already said, usually for emphasis

revival – renewed interest. In the book, it refers to a period of renewed interest in religion, characterized by a series of meetings with highly emotional sermons and songs, held in a church or sometimes in a tent.

sanctuary – This word can have different meanings: a place of refuge and safety, a holy place.

scudding – moving fast and in a straight line, usually driven by wind

skirmish – a brief and unplanned fight during a war; usually involves small numbers of troops

sporadic (adj.) – scattered or isolated, occurring at irregular intervals *surreptitious (adj.)* – describes something done in secret

tannins – a reddish acid found in many plants

thicket – a dense group of bushes or trees

tussling – engaging in a vigorous scuffle or fight

HISTORICAL FIGURES MENTIONED IN THE BOOK

(Ranks are given as they were at the Battle of Shiloh.)

CONFEDERATE OFFICERS:

General Pierre Gustave Toutant Beauregard

Usually referred to as *P.G.T. Beauregard*, General Beauregard had the distinction of leading the Confederate troops in the first battle of the Civil War, with the attack on and capture of the federal Fort Sumter in the harbor of Charleston, South Carolina.

General Albert Sidney Johnston

General Johnston, who was killed at Shiloh, was the highest-ranking casualty of the Civil War, including both North and South.

UNION OFFICERS:

Major General Don Carlos Buell

Buell brought with him three divisions consisting of about 20,000 men to reinforce the Union troops at Shiloh. He was relieved of command in October, 1862. As a former slave owner, some thought him a southern sympathizer.

Major General Ulysses S. Grant

Grant was promoted to Lieutenant General before the Civil War ended, and in 1866, after the end of the war, he was made General of the Army. He was elected President of the United States in 1869.

Brigadier General William Tecumseh Sherman

Sherman was promoted to Major General before the Civil War ended and was made Commanding General of the Army after Grant became president.

Brigadier General William Hervey Lamme Wallace

Usually referred to as *W.H.L.Wallace*, Wallace was a new division commander when he was at Shiloh. His men held off six hours of repeated assaults by the Confederates at the Hornet's Nest. Only after his division was completely surrounded did he order a withdrawal. He was mortally wounded during the battle and died three days later.

DISCUSSION QUESTIONS

1. Do you find it helpful or interesting that the story is told from the points of view of both Luke and Ethan? Why would the author give you two points of view?

2. How are Ethan and Luke alike, and how are they different?

3. Whose story do you think it is for the most part and why?

4. Not everyone agrees on why the Civil War (1861-1865) was fought. Even Luke and Ethan seem to have different perspectives. What do you think the Civil War was really about?

5. Many of the characters in this book do not directly appear in the story. For example, Ethan's parents, Luke's parents, and Uncle John. Why do you think the author brings them in to the story?

6. The songs that the Union troops sing around the campfire are all songs written before the Battle of Shiloh. Many other songs were written during the later years of the Civil War. Can you think of any that you might know?

7. Can you imagine what happened when Luke returns home? Can you write the scene in which he returns to his family?

8. Is the grown-up Luke different from the boy Luke? If so, how? Are the two alike in some ways? If so, how?

9. Does the poem by Rimbaud at the beginning of the book help you understand the theme of the book?

10. What role does nature play in the novel?

11. Union troops are buried and, whenever possible, identified at Shiloh National Cemetery, while Confederate troops lie in mass unmarked graves? Why do you suppose that happened?

12. Has war changed very much since the Civil War in the 19th century? If so, how? What are some of the ways in which people try to avoid wars today?

CPSIA information can be obtained
at www.ICGtesting.com
Printed in the USA
BVHW09s1037101018
529785BV00019B/2353/P